'Louise Doughty writes about people who don't usually get written about ... every bit as skilled as her contemporaries, her writing has a pessimistic edge which makes her books all the funnier. *Dance With Me* is a painfully accurate record of mating rituals and dating nightmares.'　　Emma Hagestadt, *Independent*

'The reader becomes engaged in the disorientating twists of a psychological thriller ... these build up with nailbiting tension to a bravura climax ... Above all, her creation of highly believable and likable female characters seems to come as naturally as breathing.'　　　　　　　　Katie Owen, *Sunday Telegraph*

'Louise Doughty combines elegance of style with sharp observation and a tender sympathy for human fallibility ... tense, stirring, and often very funny, this novel maintains a cracking pace almost to the end ... the writing is crisp and delightful throughout.'　　　　　　　Isabel Raphael, *Ham & High*

'Economical prose packing each page with finely-balanced action and psychological insight ... a ghost story with a difference. Excellent.'　　　　Rajinder Lawley, *Whats On in Birmingham*

'*Dance With Me* is a book dotted with vivid observational set pieces, cunningly slotted together ... Doughty is a good writer, deft with observational details ... This book does dance with you. It holds you, leads you, and twirls you about.'
　　　　　　　　　　　　　　　　Lynne Truss, *Sunday Times*

'An irresistible psychological thriller and cracking follow-up to the acclaimed *Crazy Paving*.'　　　　Murphy Williams, *Elle*

Louise Doughty is a writer and broadcaster. In 1990, she was the recipient of an Ian St. James Award for a short story and a Radio Times Drama Award for her first play, *Maybe*, later broadcast on Radio Three. Her second play, *The Koala Bear Joke*, was broadcast on Radio Four in 1994.

Her first novel, *Crazy Paving*, was published to critical acclaim in 1995 and was shortlisted for three awards, including the John Llewelyn Rhys Prize. *Dance With Me* is her second novel.

DANCE WITH ME

Louise Doughty

TOUCHSTONE

LONDON · SYDNEY · NEW YORK · TOKYO · SINGAPORE · TORONTO

First published in Great Britain by Touchstone, 1996
This paperback edition first published by Touchstone, 1996
An imprint of Simon & Schuster Ltd
A Viacom Company

Simon & Schuster Ltd
West Garden Place
Kendal Street
London
W2 2AQ

Simon & Schuster of Australia Pty Ltd
Sydney

Quotation from *Tropic of Cancer* © The Estate of Henry Miller.
Reproduced with kind permission of Curtis Brown Group Ltd, London.

A CIP catalogue record for this book is available form the British Library.

ISBN 0-684-81760-8

Printed and bound in Great Britain by Cox & Wyman, Reading

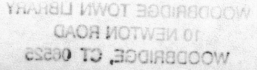

For
all my women friends
but especially
my sister
Rachel

It may be that we are doomed, that there is no hope for us, *any of us*, but if that is so then let us set up a last agonizing, bloodcurdling howl, a screech of defiance, a war whoop! . . . Let the dead eat the dead. Let us living ones dance about the rim of the crater, a last expiring dance. But a dance!

Henry Miller
Tropic of Cancer

March is the month of Expectation.
The things we do not know –
The Persons of Prognostication
Are coming now –
We try to show becoming firmness –
But pompous Joy
Betrays us, as his first Betrothal
Betrays a Boy.

Emily Dickinson

1

*L*ove is easy. Love is cheap. Any idiot can do it. You don't have to have brains or looks or money – you don't even have to be a nice person. Hitler fell in love – so did Stalin and Genghis Khan and Vlad the Impaler. An amoeba would weep at *Brief Encounter* (if an amoeba could weep, that is). I don't resent people who are in love. I just wish they wouldn't walk around as if it's an achievement.

So. Let us have the facts. On the first of March, a year ago, I met Peter. By the end of March, he was dead. He was killed in a road accident three weeks after our first date. He was driving along the Watford by-pass, going at roughly sixty miles an hour, when a lorry which was pulling out of a side road ahead blew a tyre, slammed on the brakes and skidded. A van in front of Peter went into the lorry. Peter went into the van. He was killed outright. The van driver was trapped for three hours; the lorry driver unscathed. It was nobody's fault.

Why Peter was driving along the Watford by-pass at eight o'clock that night was a mystery to me – although I found out later. I was waiting for him in a pub in Mill Hill at the time. We had arranged to meet at seven.

Several days after his death, I received a polite and sympathetic letter from a solicitor called Mr Jay Benby, inviting me to a meet him at his offices in the West End at my earliest possible convenience. After coffee and condolences, he informed me carefully that one week before the accident, Peter had altered his will, making me the sole beneficiary. I was now a wealthy woman. Mr Jay Benby pronounced these two words with a slight drawl – as if wealth was something it was necessary to be a little sarcastic about, perhaps in an effort to reduce its potency. He was leaning back in a leather-padded chair. On the wall behind him was a poster print of a landscape done with broad strokes in browns and oranges. It was hung in a cheap glass clip-frame which struck a note of incongruity in an office which was mainly old-fashioned (wood, carpets, ticking clock). The rest of the office said, *trust me*. The glass clip-frame with its burnt river and orange mountains and brownish sky said, *don't believe a word*.

I looked at him and said, 'What?'

Benby paused. 'You are the sole beneficiary. You are a wealthy woman.'

The second time round, it occurred to me that the drawl was not so much on the word wealthy as *woman*. I wondered if women were also something Benby felt it necessary to be sarcastic about. He was around thirty but had an air of being older. His hair was thinning and the flesh on his face a little slack. He was nicely dressed –

expensive shirt, silk tie – but it was already clear what he would be like at sixty. Here was a man whose future was made of concrete. Nothing unexpected would be happening to him. Perhaps, as a consequence, he did not believe in the unexpected – which would mean, of necessity, that he did not believe in me. A man dies a week after rewriting his will. No wonder Benby was drawling.

'The estate includes Mr Attwell's house on Lake View,' Benby said, leaning forward in his chair and resting his forearms on his desk. In front of him, there was a blotting pad with brass corners. Next to it bobbled a green plastic man on a spring, with two biros and a pencil protruding from his head. 'I can arrange for it to be put on the market, unless you are thinking of inhabiting it yourself of course. His effects . . .'

I shook my head, playing for time. Benby didn't know it, but I was living there already.

*

Iris sits at her desk and types. In front of her, the PC chunters softly. There is something about the noise that reminds Iris of aeroplanes; the sound of an aeroplane waiting on the runway; a constant, expectant, slightly terrifying whoosh. Her friend and sometime associate George Leary hates the sound. George tells her that all PC-users are living in the Dark Ages and that Mac technology is taking over the world and as far as he's concerned she might as well go back to the abacus. But then George is a bit of a prat; a prat with a mouse fetish. Iris is a function-button girl.

The noise irritates her too. She didn't notice it when she worked from home. Her workroom there was too full of other sounds – cars going past, the wind in the trees outside her block of flats, a neighbour's radio – buzzes which said, *this is where you live*. Now that she is installed in this rented, echoey office, the hum of her PC has taken on a completely different tone; something to do with the size of the room, perhaps, or the fact that it is half-empty. Here, she is aware of all sorts of things.

She had to rent somewhere, though. She was going mad at home.

She is trying to write a marketing plan. It is dull as ditch water. The client is someone she has been working for for years, the managing director of a small chemical company in Middlesex. She did a set-up job for them when they first got going and they've used her ever since. Systems set-ups are her speciality and with the Internet, the field is exploding. She is running training courses every other week. Information Consultant, says her business card, although her regulars know that she does some marketing and report-writing as well.

It annoys her that she is not yet at the stage where she feels able to turn down these deadwood jobs. She has been self-employed for several years but still suffers from a seemingly congenital inability to say no to anything. She is on her own. She worries about money all the time.

However much work is coming in, there is always the ache and weight of responsibility.

The current job is irritating her in particular. She knows that the managing director – who has ginger hair and is called Mr James – thinks that he has been using Iris for too long and someone else could do it better. Iris doesn't want to work for him any more but continues to do it and undercharge him as well, out of some weird sense of superstition. It would seem bad luck to dump James Chemical & Hygiene Co Ltd, in the same way that it would seem bad luck to tread on a spider. She suspects they still hire her for the same reason. As a result, there is an edge of bad feeling all round. She thinks their product mediocre. They find her marketing plans unexciting. They exchange Christmas cards each year as if they were old friends.

Iris has just typed, *What profit a company if it gains a greater percentage share of the market but loseth the competitive edge that gave it the profits in the first place?* She stops and frowns. Mr James left school at fourteen and, as a result, likes his marketing plans peppered with references to Shakespeare. They hurt Iris's professional pride. They give her the mental equivalent of a bunion.

She pushes herself away from her desk then presses both of her shoulders back, arching her spine. Then she lifts her hands and wobbles them from side to side, shaking out her fingers. Iris is terrified of two things: back pain and repetitive strain injury. She has a long-term pension for the self-employed but no sick cover. She would work with a broken leg. She hauled herself into her office throughout

5

a two-week bout of flu in January. But if she develops RSI or back pain she will only be cured if she sacks herself. They are the only things she can think of which might finish her off.

But she must plough on. It is 7.10pm and the rest of the building is in darkness.

She uses the cursor to scroll upwards. It is lazy of her to read through from the top without printing out but she wants to get to the end of the first draft before her brain packs in altogether. The white letters on the screen flash and blur. It gives her the sick sensation you get by watching a goods train rattle past when you're sitting on a station platform. Her eyes flicker.

Iris. Her name is neat, appropriate. It is her job to look. Computer information always comes through the eye – there is rarely any need to listen. Appropriate, then – and not just distasteful as she had thought at school. Iris; a technical term for a piece of coloured jelly. In her second-year Maths class, there had been a girl called Marietta Twigg who screamed every time she heard the phrase *keep your eyes peeled.* The boys used to sneak up to her and whisper it, just to watch her scamper over to the corner and cower there with her hands over her face, squealing like a rabbit.

Keep your eyes peeled. Iris's eyes were permanently peeled, wide open, gathering information like a whale sucking in plankton.

As she reaches the top of the document, the cursor bumps against the ceiling of the screen and her machine gives a small dull clunk which it repeats grumpily for the duration of the second it takes to lift her finger off the button. The machine is quicker than she is, albeit blind.

*

So. Who am I? I am twenty-seven years old. I am tall, with legs that tend to muscular but neat hips which are the envy of my women friends. My hair is short. My mouth is large; my skin smooth. I tan easily. I have the kind of face that you would call interesting, if you were being polite – a little odd, if you were not. It has been observed that I have a model's features – you know, not conventionally beautiful but would look good when photographed in the right light. This, frankly, is bullshit. I don't look good photographed in any light. What I look is different. Large mouth, then, large eyes – straight, slender nose, short cropped hair with floppy fringe – *something sparkly*, a man once told me, and I think it was the nicest compliment I have ever had. There is something sparkly about me. Once in a while men catch on to the sparkle and become obsessed.

My real name is Felicity (another Fact) but somewhere around the age of three or four I acquired the nickname Bet; a corruption, perhaps, from a term of endearment like *pet* or *petal* – or maybe it was short for something; Beth, Bettina, better, betrothal, *bête noire*. Betrayal.

It was probably my father. *Felicity* would have been my mother's choice – my mother, who liked all things flowery. Any new purchase for her or myself or the bathroom would

7

be justified with the phrase, *but it's so pretty*. She must have been overjoyed when – after thirty hours of very unpretty labour – a baby girl popped out. Even a baby girl as strapping as myself could still be prettified somehow, in my case with endless streams of ribbons and *bourdre anglaise* and puff-sleeved little dresses. God knows what she would have done if I had been a boy.

My father died when I was six so memories of him are hazy – but I remember someone big and loose, someone who swung me around a lot. I remember weeding the garden beside him dressed in denim dungarees, my hands black, soil smeared on my forehead. Do we inherit distinct characteristics from our parents? I certainly did. They could not be more distinct if I was piebald. From my mother I inherited a certain petulance when I am thwarted and a fondness for silk. My father bequeathed to me my height, my toughness and my proficiency with a trowel. I may be *felicitous* – but I am also a good *bet*.

*

Iris stops, her hands frozen above the keyboard, her back stiff. She listens. There is no sound. She listens some more and, while she listens, tells herself not to be so stupid, to get on with her marketing plan, to stop thinking about the fact she works in an ancient, half-deserted building and her office is the only one which is occupied on her corridor.

She will not lock the door. That would be giving in.

She continues typing for a moment or so but the fear

8

has started up in her belly and she knows it is no use. With a sigh, she rises from her seat. At the door, she pauses, wondering whether or not to go out into the corridor and stand in the darkness, defiantly, as she sometimes does, to prove to herself that she is not a character in a made-for-TV thriller who is about to make That Fatal Mistake. Which is more silly – the Mistake, or the determination not to make it?

She is too busy for any of that nonsense tonight. She has this damn thing to finish. She clicks the Yale lock on with a noise that seems unreasonably loud, then returns to her desk and recommences typing, furiously. Later, she will have to get from her office to the exit but she can manage that as long as she does it quickly. Shadows only exist if you notice them. Shut your eyes and run.

*

After I left Benby's office, I strode swiftly down the corridor, past the doors to other offices which contained other Benbys (being sarcastic to other unexpected heiresses no doubt), past a hot-drinks machine at the top of the stairs, past the receptionist on the floor below who grinned at me as I swept by. I was breathing hard and biting my lip. I felt as though everybody on the planet knew the secrets of my heart – everyone, that is, except myself.

As I reached the ground floor, my feet slowed down. I paused on the threshold of the building. Stone steps led down to the street. I flopped down them, one by one, and with each step I sank a little lower, both physically and metaphorically. By the time I had reached the bottom, I had reached the bottom.

I took a few steps out into the street. It was a typical March day. Bleeding freezing. A grey wind chuffed horizontally down the street, lifting the corner of my coat to peer underneath. I felt its cold fingers grope around my legs. The sky was dense with cloud.

Just before the curb there was a lamp-post, an old-fashioned wrought-iron one with a fluted surface. I took a step towards it, then stopped. Then, gently, I leant my forehead against the rough, frozen metal and closed my eyes. Peter, I thought. *Peter*. After our first date, I had woken with a hangover. He had laid his hand on my forehead and his palm had been cool balm. Peter.

After a moment or so, I stood back and glanced around. The street surrounded a quiet square and was almost empty. A few yards away, there was a red telephone box.

Inside, it smelt of stale smoke and car exhaust fumes. I plumped down my handbag on the little shelf and pulled out my address book.

The phone was answered after four rings.

'Sophie?' I asked.

'Yes.'

'It's me, Bet. I've just come from the solicitor's office. I've found out what it was. You're not going to believe this . . .' I drew breath. I had begun to cry. 'Everything. He's left everything to me. Every penny. What am I going to do?'

There was a pause on the other end of the line.

I snuffled and wiped my nose with the back of my hand. 'Is Alex out?' I asked.

'No,' she said. 'He's outside dealing with someone. I'm in the office.'

'What am I going to do?'

'Come over,' she said. 'Come over now.'

Sophie and Alex were Peter's best friends. I had known them only a few weeks but it felt like years. I had completed the foursome like the missing piece of a jigsaw puzzle, Peter said. We were both tall and dark – Sophie and Alex were short and fair. Peter and I dressed in suits and shirts – Sophie and Alex habitually wore jeans and trainers. We were like two bundles sat in either saucer on a pair of old-fashioned scales. Before I came along it had been very unbalanced, Peter said. I was so charmed by my own appositeness that it did not occur to me to wonder what had drawn them together as friends in the first place.

At the funeral, they stood either side of me, like sentinels. I was bewildered. I felt very small, and very grateful. They introduced me to everyone as, 'Peter's girlfriend'. There were a lot of people to introduce – the crematorium was packed. Two pale grey elderly people came up and shook my hand and it was only after they had blundered away that Sophie whispered to me, 'His aunt and uncle'. I observed their departing backs with interest. Peter had been raised by them.

Apart from that, there were a whole host of people Sophie called, 'Business associates'. Men in suits, mostly, although there was also a smattering of women, all of them with lots of hair and nail varnish. At one point, one of the women came up to me and gripped my arm. Her nails pressed into the sleeve of my black linen jacket. 'You probably didn't . . .' she said shakily, and I saw that her eyelashes were heavy with huge teardrops, each containing a swirl of mascara which swelled swimmingly, dangerously.

I didn't know what to say, so I nodded.

She returned my nod.

Noiselessly, Alex came up behind me and took hold of my elbow. His grip was protectively firm as he lead me to a waiting car. Confused, I looked back at the woman, my head turned awkwardly because Alex was guiding me towards the open passenger door. She was gazing after me, standing quite still and clutching a piece of blue tissue. She lifted it briefly. My last sight of her was of that small flash of blue, then I turned back and climbed in.

Sophie was already sitting in the rear seat, leaning back with a sigh. As Alex climbed into the driver's seat and slammed the door behind him she said, 'Well that all went off okay, thank God.'

As the car reversed, to turn down the long gravel drive, several people who were still standing and talking lifted black-gloved hands to wave at us. I lifted mine, automatically, as I spoke. 'Shouldn't we have organised a wake of some sort, sandwiches and tea, or something? I've never been to a funeral without a wake. I would have liked to have met the aunt.'

I saw Alex glance into the rearview mirror. 'I don't want

to sound mysterious,' he said slowly, 'but there are quite a few people in Peter's life who didn't really see eye-to-eye, if you know what I mean. A wake might have been a little tricky.'

Sophie leaned forward from the back seat and laid a soft, plump hand on my right shoulder. 'How are you feeling?' she asked, very gently.

'Oh . . .' I said, biting my lip and turning my head away to stare out of the side window. 'Oh . . . you know.'

I loved Sophie and Alex's place. Their surroundings were as plump and blonde as they were; not my style – but that only made it all the more attractive. Their kitchen was wide and shiny; pale Swedish wood, white marble. In the sitting-room there was a low, cream-coloured three-piece suite which was so soft that the cushions rose up about your ears as you sank into it. 'Dreadful for your back,' Peter had whispered to me, the first time we went round.

'What?' Sophie had called over her shoulder, on her way out to the kitchen to fetch the tea.

'Wonderful you're back!' Peter called out, and squeezed my hand.

Sophie and Alex had been on holiday to Tunisia. The coffee table in front of us was stacked with an ominously high pile of photographs in paper wallets, newly collected from the chemist.

'Someday my prints will come!' sang Peter as he reached forward.

'You're such an idiot,' said Sophie, as she returned with

13

a white china teapot. 'Does this kid know what she's let herself in for?'

The front door slammed.

'Alex! Alex!' Sophie called out. 'We're in here and Peter's brought someone with him and she's far too nice for him.'

Alex entered, all stocky frame and big hands and lopsided, bounding grin. He swooped on Sophie. '*Anybody*'s too good for Peter!' Then he bent her over backwards and buried his head in the side of her neck, growling.

She shrieked. 'Get off me and go and be polite!'

He dropped her so quickly she nearly toppled over. Then he turned to me, reaching out with a muscular arm. I raised myself a few inches, a little awkwardly. He grasped my hand but did not shake it. Instead, he looked straight into my face and said without any hint of a twinkle, 'Has he been rude about our sofa yet?'

'Of course he has,' Sophie was saying as she knelt the other side of the coffee table and lifted the teapot. 'Peter couldn't possibly bring somebody round here without being rude about the sofa.'

Later I was treated to the guided tour. Alex and Peter had gone out to the back garden to look at rose bushes, which they were both interested in, apparently. Sophie and I were left to bond in the way that women always are, based on the assumption that your common gender gives you plenty to talk about.

'So what do you do?' Sophie asked as we walked back into the kitchen, she with fistfuls of crockery.

'PR,' I replied vaguely, feeling a little awkward because I

was not helping her carry things – torn between politeness and my political objections to the implication that that is how a woman's courtesy is defined. 'I'm between jobs actually, freelancing. I've got some work from a fashion company but it's only really part-time, lunches I can charge to the client and so on. I should really sort myself out with more work but I've got some money left over so it's hard to summon up any urgency.'

'Fashion,' Sophie was saying, divesting herself of cups and saucers onto the immaculate white surface of the kitchen bar. 'Interesting. Let's give you the guided tour.'

She turned and gestured me out into the hall. 'We'll leave out the office, that's the boring bit.' They ran their own business selling accessories to people who owned boats, Sophie explained as she led me upstairs. There was an office adjacent to the kitchen and a huge shed in the back garden with sailing gear and all sorts of other things.

The upstairs was exactly what I had expected: a king-size bed in the master bedroom with a duvet the size of a small continent; a peachy bathroom with toiletries decanted into misty glass bottles. I realised why I liked the house, and them, so much. They fitted. They fitted each other and then together they fitted into their home. All this softness and cleanness and warmth – it was so right for them and they so right for each other. It's rare, after all, to come across people who really suit each other – so rare that it's actually quite charming, even if you know you would rather be dead than live like that yourself. These are people, I thought, who will have happy lives.

It was while we were in the bathroom that Sophie had an attack of self-deprecation. 'We're rather fluffy, aren't we, me and Alex ... and all this ...' she added, waving her arm around. The curtains were a fresh peach and white stripe. Somebody more twee would have chosen flowers. They weren't that bad.

'Oh, you're not that bad,' I said, and Sophie smiled warmly.

There was a moment's pause. Sophie was looking at me. Her eyes were a light hazel brown, round and soft. Her gaze was protective. 'You like Peter, don't you?' she said gently.

I bit my lower lip and looked down at the floor. Sophie was no fool. 'Yes,' I murmured sheepishly. 'I do.' I decided to fish. 'I suppose you've seen a few come and go?'

Sophie was nodding. 'Oh yes.' She paused. 'Mostly with larger breasts than you.'

I opened my mouth in a silent laugh. She leaned forward and placed a hand on my forearm. 'The four of us are going to go out together very soon,' she said, smiling, 'and we're going to have a *really* good time.'

Downstairs, the boys had returned from the garden and Peter was rubbing his hands together in the gesture which I already knew meant, *time to go.*

Sophie and Alex went into the kitchen while Peter and I collected our coats from the hall. As Peter helped me on with mine, he ran a finger down my spine. I turned to him and smiled. Our glances collided and my stomach folded in on itself. I turned away from him, to recover my

16

composure, and took a few steps towards the kitchen, to say goodbye.

Sophie and Alex were emerging together. Sophie was first, holding a yellow plastic duty-free bag. She was talking to Alex over her shoulder and didn't notice how close to them I was. I heard her say, 'Freelance something or other.' At the same time, she turned her head and saw me. A broad smile spread across her features. 'Don't drink it all at once,' she said, holding up the bag. As I took it from her, I glanced up at Alex. He was not looking at me. He was looking past me, at Peter. The expression on his face was one of self-satisfaction.

They waved us off from the front doorstep.

'I like them,' I said, as we swung round the corner, out of the cul-de-sac and onto the main road. The duty-free bag was sitting between my feet. The bottles in it clanked together. Peter was gazing straight ahead. He broke into a smile. 'They like you.'

We pulled up at a set of traffic lights and Peter took advantage of the pause to lean over and pull me towards him by placing a hand on the back of my head, landing a plump kiss on my mouth. 'They're my best friends,' he said as he sat back, 'and you were absolutely charming.' The lights changed. He grabbed and shook the gearstick. 'And when we get home, I'm going to shag the living daylights out of you.'

I let out a yelp of laughter as the car surged forward.

The drive from the crematorium to Alex and Sophie's

house took less than an hour. For most of the time we drove in silence; a calm, companionable silence, the silence of soldiers returning from the front. We had not discussed what we would do after the cremation but all three of us seemed to assume that they would take me back to their place, for a drink or something. On the way there, we drove past the end of Peter's road. I craned my neck to get a glimpse of his house, my house now. Odd to think that inside it were my belongings: my shoes dropped carelessly into the alcove behind the front door; my make-up bag squatting on the bathroom shelf; my laundry in occupation of the washing-machine, steaming softly in a crumpled wet heap because I had not had time to hang it out before Alex and Sophie picked me up. My presence in the house had never seemed apparent when Peter was there as well. Now there was no Peter, only the colonial spread of my possessions – the incongruity of me.

I had not spent a night in my own flat since the day that Peter and I had met. I had not spent many daylight hours there either. The immediacy of our cohabitation had never been discussed. It had just happened. We met at a party. I went back to his house with him and spent the night. The following morning, as I was standing by his bed buttoning my shirt, he said, 'What time can you come back?'

He was still in bed, turned sideways with his head propped up on one elbow and the bedclothes strewn over him as if he was advertising aftershave. I glanced up and then returned to my buttons. 'Not sure,' I said. 'I've got to see somebody this afternoon.'

He sat up and reached out, catching me by one arm and pulling until I tumbled clumsily onto the bed. He gathered me into his chest. It smelt of hair, sweat, sex – the smell that you only get with the combination of all three. I lifted my free hand and laid it against his warm, rough cheek, breathing him in; half sick with wanting him.

When I let myself in through my own front door, my small square flat seemed small, and square; somewhere which belonged to somebody who was not me. I was carrying a couple of items of post which I had picked up in the hall downstairs. I turned them over and surveyed the envelopes without curiosity, then tossed them onto the table.

It was gone noon. I should have spent the morning preparing for my meeting, an early afternoon tea – at my expense – with somebody who might or might not give me work. There was only just time to have a bath and change. A lot of money was at stake and normally I would have been nervous.

The curtains were still closed from the previous evening. I went over and flung them open, then looked around. The woman who was not me had painted the walls an anodyne magnolia colour and hung up a couple of Mexican rugs. There was a second-hand table, brown and beaten, around which were ranged three wooden chairs which had each been painted a different colour – red, orange, green – to pick up tones from the rug which hung on the adjacent wall. Interesting I thought; stop; hesitate; go. This woman has a sense of humour.

I wandered around like a car crash victim who has lost her memory and is learning about herself for the first time.

When the phone rang, I jumped. It was Peter.

'Hi. You got back all right.' Hearing his voice was like having treacle tipped over me, slowly.

'Yes.'

'Good.'

'My flat is . . . weird. My flat is weird.'

'I know. My house seemed really strange as soon as you'd left, as though somebody had emptied half the contents out. Why do you have to see somebody this afternoon and when are you coming back?'

My voice had a catch in it as I answered, 'Tonight.'

In the bath, I soaped my soft, unusual body – the one I had acquired overnight. It intrigued me. I was keen to get acquainted.

In the following three weeks I returned to the flat four or maybe five times, just to check the post and pick up clothing. I was using a pager to ring my answer machine in case there were any work calls, then returning them from Peter's house.

Peter's house had swallowed me whole. It's fair to say that when I first saw it, I was horrified. Peter did not have much in the way of taste – a personality defect which I thought rather charming, priding myself on how

I would bring him gradually round to Mexican rugs and coloured chairs. The word to describe Peter's house was *functional*. He had an old-fashioned belief, shared by my mother, incidentally, that second-hand furniture is somehow tacky and a bit grim, and that included antiques. (My mother took it one stage further, believing, I think, that owning other people's cast-offs of any sort was a sign of a weak character or lack of moral fibre.) I never identified the source of any of Peter's stuff – brass light fittings and a fair amount of teak. The phrase which came closest was *anonymous expensive*. It was only gradually that I began to comprehend that it described a great deal of Peter quite apart from his furniture.

Within a few days, he had cleared out a small room next to the bedroom which had previously contained the only junk he seemed to possess – a set of encyclopaedias, a VCR that Peter said was broken and an exercise bike. 'Your room,' he had said firmly, edging in a small, teak, drop-leaf table. 'You've got to have somewhere to make phone calls from and build up a client list.'

I watched from the doorway, amused. 'I don't think I'm going to be self-employed for that long,' I said. 'I'm only doing it to bide my time. As soon as something else comes up I'll take it.' He frowned. I couldn't tell whether it was at me or at the effort of negotiating the table into position. 'I don't have the necessary psychological stamina,' I explained, as he turned back to me. 'And you have some dirt on your nose.'

He walked towards me and presented his face. I moistened a finger and rubbed at the small grubby smear, something he had picked up while moving the table. Then I put my finger into his mouth. He leaned his body weight forward so that I was pressed up against the door frame. I could feel the ridge of it in my back. His face was very close to mine and with a mouth full of finger he mumbled, 'You . . . are in bad trouble . . .'

He was right, as it turned out, but not in the way he meant. And the trouble in store for me on the floor of Peter's spare room that brutally innocent afternoon was nothing compared with the trouble waiting for him on the Watford by-pass less than a month down the line. But which of us could have predicted that? I didn't even predict the attack of cystitis which struck me two days later, although considering what we had been up to and my sexual history it was very stupid of me not to have foreseen that one.

I am prone to cystitis. It is one of the occupational hazards of being promiscuous – and I am promiscuous as hell.

2

I thought that perhaps I was through with Benby but had a sinking feeling, nonetheless, that he was far from through with me. Peter had apparently explained to him that he had no next of kin, as such, so he wanted Benby to be his executor; an unusual move, Benby said, but not extraordinary. (I was desperate to know what Benby *would* consider extraordinary. Arriving at work to find an orchestra of mice playing *La Dolce Vita* on his blotting pad, perhaps?) As a result, it was Benby's responsibility to get the paperwork together and file it with the Probate Registry. Young Benby proved to be very keen on the word responsibility and used it against me, like blackmail. He hated to trouble me at what must be a very difficult time, he said when he rang, but he was sure I understood it was necessary for him to fulfil his *responsibilities*.

It was not until the third or fourth of these phone calls that I began to smell a rat. By then, I had told him that I had moved into Peter's house, to sort out his effects.

Benby seemed very interested in this information. 'Perhaps,' he suggested lightly, 'I should come over and pick up some of Mr Atwell's papers. There is probably some paperwork there, I gather. It may be of relevance, for the Grant of Probate.' When I didn't respond, he began to patronise me, which was a mistake. 'I am sure you have quite enough on your plate, Miss Walker, Felicity if I may. His personal belongings, clothing and so on. The paperwork could just be left I'm sure.'

Bollocks to this, I thought. Nobody has called me Felicity in years, let alone Felicity-if-I-may. And who is *Miss* Walker? This guy is living in the Dark Ages. 'I think I can manage,' I responded, a little tartly. Then I played my trump card. 'Actually, right now, I think what I really need is to be alone.'

The police turned up the next morning. Benby was no snail.

I was still in my dressing gown, or rather Peter's. I had been up late the previous night, wandering around the house, turning lights on and off and talking to Peter in my head as if his death was one of his little games, an extra special one, designed to tease me extra-specially.

In the morning I slept in, waking to the rectangle of bruised light which shone through Peter's thin, dark purple curtains. As usual, there was the brief struggle with my surroundings, the information drip-feeding itself into my befuddled brain: I was not going to work because I was between jobs; a few weeks ago I had met a new bloke; he was dead; I was living in his house . . .

I hadn't quite come to terms with the timer on Peter's

thermostat so the house was always freezing when I woke. My first task was to pull on his old silk dressing-gown and the Chinese slippers I had brought from my flat, then pad out to the landing to turn the central heating and the hot water on full. Then I would go to the toilet, sitting shivering with my arms wrapped across my chest, before scampering back to bed and huddling beneath the soft feather duvet which still smelled of Peter, rubbing myself against the sheets to recover my own rapidly fading body warmth.

That morning, I was on my way back to bed when the doorbell rang. There had been few callers since the accident: a neighbour returning a garden fork, a window-cleaner wanting payment. The neighbour knew that Peter had died and peered at me with undisguised curiosity. The window-cleaner had snatched the tenner from my hand and stalked off down the drive without so much as a raised eyebrow, which made me wonder how many other women in dressing-gowns had paid Peter's window-cleaning bill.

Through the hall window I could see the car parked in the drive, a small two-door job. I felt a brief flush of relief. They had only sent round a couple of bobbies to do a bit of routine questioning. Nothing heavy.

I opened the door to two men who seemed improbably large to have arrived in such a small vehicle. Radios crackled fiercely on their chests. Instinctively, I drew the dressing-gown around my chest and tightened the sash, probably because that is what women always do in television series when the police arrive on their doorstep.

'Miss Walker?' one asked.

I nodded.

In the sitting-room, they gestured for me to sit on the sofa. They both removed their hats. One of them perched himself on the arm of a nearby chair. The other remained standing, looking around the room. I wanted to offer them coffee (I was dying for one myself) but that would have seemed too clichéd for words.

PC Sitting Down questioned me while PC Standing Up took notes.

How long had I known Peter?

At the answer, the one taking notes paused briefly before writing it down.

Was I surprised to find myself the sole beneficiary of his will?

Yes, of course, I answered. *And that Benby is a two-faced blabbermouth* I added silently.

Did I know what Peter did for a living? Had I ever met any of his business associates? The people at the crematorium, had I ever seen any of them before, or since?

As soon as I could get away with it, I interrupted, my voice taking on a slightly girlish tone, 'You're not suggesting . . .'

The sitting policeman gave an unfooled smile. No, he was not suggesting that Mr Atwell's death was in any way suspicious. That possibility had of course been looked into. No, it wasn't that.

What then?

They persisted with the questions for a while, until they

got around to the meat of it. They wanted to look round the house.

I felt like telling them to sod off, even though I knew they probably had a magistrate's warrant in their pocket, Benby being such a stickler for propriety. Peter's mysteries were my property. If anybody was going to unravel anything it was going to be me – me who knew about the way he kissed, me who had pillow-fought with him on no fewer than three occasions. Who were these large men in their navy blue uniforms and their silly little car? What business was it of theirs?

Instead, I waved a hand loosely in the direction of the stairs. Be my guest.

While they were gone, their footsteps tramping heavily, I lay back on the sofa and closed my eyes.

I had realised very early on that whatever Peter was into, it was dodgy. He had always been vague and secretive about his work; leaving the house to 'go and see someone', shutting his study door to make phone calls. It could have been anything from tax evasion to drug dealing, for all I knew, or cared. I didn't mind that there were parts of him I didn't know about. To be honest, it turned me on. I knew that something must have made Benby suspicious. The amount Peter had left? Me? I also knew that if the policemen were going to work through the desk in Peter's study and the filing cabinet next to it, they would find nothing other than household bills, insurance policies and notes about socks and jumpers from his aunt. I knew because in the past week I had been through every single drawer and every file. There were no clues there.

There was, however, enough to keep the police cheerfully occupied for nearly an hour. After that, one of them came down and explained that they wanted to take a few things away with them and was it alright? Upstairs, I could hear the other throwing folders into a cardboard box.

They went away happy enough. I watched them from behind the plain net curtains of the sitting-room as they loaded up the back seat of the little car. Then I laughed softly to myself as they folded their bulky forms into the front seats, like Keystone Cops. Once they were inside with the doors shut, the one in the driver's seat loosened his tie. The other scratched behind his ear before he reached back for his seatbelt. They were talking to each other. Their expressions were bored.

After they had gone, I phoned Alex and Sophie. I had not spoken to them for a couple of days.

'Shit,' said Alex, when I told him about the police. I was hoping that Sophie would answer the phone, not him. 'How many boxes did you say?'

'Two,' I replied, 'one on top of the other. But it was only the stuff in the study, there wasn't anything important in there.'

There was the slightest of pauses. 'How do you know?'

I batted back, pause for pause. 'I've been through everything in there already.'

Almost imperceptibly, I heard Alex inhale, slowly. His

thoughts were inaudible, but I could sense his mind computing at the speed of light.

'Alex,' I said. 'Don't you think it's time that you and Sophie told me a bit more about Peter? I know you knew him much longer than I did and I'm hardly in a position to start complaining when you've both been so nice to me but I'm not daft. And what if I decide to stay living here? Don't you think I ought to be told?'

There was a long pause. Then Alex said, 'Yes.'

'Dinner? Tonight? Why don't you come round here. I've got to go out and do some shopping anyway I've nearly used up all of Peter's tins and I'm dying for some fruit.'

'Sophie could give you a lift to Sainsbury's if you like.' He had recovered himself.

'No it's all right, I might as well make friends with Peter's Mini. I might want to keep it after all. I've never owned a car. I've had a licence for years but I've never quite got round to getting one. More trouble than it's worth.'

'Yes ... yes, quite right.' Alex was slightly too jovial now, under the circumstances. 'I'm not sure you'll get the Mini going though. God knows when Peter last drove it. Careful.'

We were both silent. Alex had meant, *careful if you haven't driven very much* but it had come out as *careful because Peter died in a car accident after all and the reason you're going to drive the Mini to the supermarket is because the BMW is in a crumpled heap somewhere awaiting pulverisation by a very large blunt object operated by a crane-driver*. There was a moment of conspiracy between us and I felt a rush of guilt for being so suspicious about Alex. Even if Peter had been up to something, it didn't automatically mean that Alex and Sophie were in on it as well.

In the supermarket, I wandered aimlessly up and down the aisles, letting the haphazard progress of my trolley pull me along. The wheels were skew-whiff. Each time I gave a small shove it twisted out of my hands in the opposite direction, zigzagging to an unsteady halt.

Supermarkets always put the fruit and veg at the entrance to give the impression of freshness as you come in. It's logical, I suppose. Would your spirits lift at a pyramid of canned peas? And that rich, bready smell around the bakery counter is not bread. It comes in canisters. They pump it out. Supermarket managers are like medieval wizards, spraying illusions.

I used to have a policy of purchasing at least one item which I had never bought before – as a matter of principle – to stave off the day when I would look in the mirror and realise I was old and staid and my life devoid of new experience or originality. But it's amazing how difficult it is. (My mother, darkly: 'The road to hell is paved with good intentions.' What sort of person says that to a child?) Supermarkets are vast, chilly aircraft hangars, so brimming with foodstuffs you could contract bulimia on the spot; yet I still find myself paralysed with unadventurousness. Do I really want that gooseberry flavour custard-style yoghurt? Wouldn't it be better to stick to fromage frais? There is nothing so bewildering as choice.

I used to have the excuse of haste: the mad dash after work when you snatch at familiar items, hungrily, banging your basket against those of your opponents; or the Saturday afternoon mayhem when the little old ladies come out of hibernation and crowd the aisles in one vast, maddening conspiracy to make sure that whatever happens you won't get home in time for the omnibus edition of *Brookside*.

But that was then. That was when I had a job and a flat and a life. As I ambled up and down the rows of light and colour, a few items clanking pathetically in my near-empty trolley, I realised that everything had changed. Peter, and his death, had suspended me. Until it was sorted out I was in a twilight zone, where he was no longer living but certainly not dead. My chance meeting with him, wine glass in hand, had overturned everything and for the time being I was belly-up, waddling up and down this sterile emporium with my empty trolley.

My urge to fill the trolley became pathological. I started to grab things from the shelves. Then, in the corner of my vision, red hulks of flesh glimmered and beckoned. I had fetched up near the meat counter and Alex was clearly a meaty sort of man. Bingo. Some nice joint. Throw it into Peter's oven and turn it once in a while. My father taught me about herbs so I'll be all right on that score. I can't cook to save my life but I can garnish like nobody's business.

The lump of beef was ludicrously heavy and wrapped in cellophane stretched tight and shiny across its muscular form. Beneath the plastic, a little blood eddied in the wrinkles of the flesh. It was the most expensive cut so it wouldn't need trimming. They'd be lucky if I rinsed it under the tap. Cooking foil? Did Peter have cooking foil? I had been rummaging through his kitchen cupboards for days but couldn't remember seeing any.

As I wheeled criss-cross style across to Baking Accessories, a single clean thought popped into my head unbidden, as pure and wicked as a thought can be. I am rich. I can buy whatever I like.

Off I went, to look at their small selection of dishes and casseroles. I wanted a big glass one, so that I could see what this lump of cow got up to while it spat and browned itself.

In the queue at the checkout, my trolley parked sideways and piled high, something odd happened. I had begun to unload. I was reaching forwards for the NEXT CUSTOMER divider and glanced towards the exit, to see that a woman had stopped dead in her tracks and was staring at me. She was wheeling a trolley crammed full of loaded plastic bags, on her way out to the car park. A toddler was sitting in the seat, turning and reaching backwards with a short chubby arm, whining for something.

The woman was around my age and height, with dark blonde hair held back at the nape of her neck by a plain band. She was wearing jeans and a sheepskin jacket. As soon as she saw I had noticed her, she turned and hurried away, pushing the trolley and shushing at her child.

It was only as I was writing out a cheque, after my food had been rung through, that I remembered where I had seen her before. She was the woman who came up and spoke to me at Peter's funeral.

Back home, it took me several relays to carry my shopping into the house and plonk it on the kitchen table. Collected, the bags seemed like a crowd of old men dressed in white plastic and crouched together, gossiping. They seemed somehow malicious. I sat down on a kitchen chair and wept.

Supermarket shopping always made me feel tearful when I got home. It was one of the few times I wanted someone else – to unload the bags with, to put the kettle on, to moan about the smallness of the fridge.

Peter and I shopped together four times. What can you learn about somebody in four trips to Sainsbury's? He hated broccoli. He bought sweetcorn in bulk. He thought it was better to get paté from the shelf in the cold counter rather than the deli section because then you could check the sell-by date.

Something in one of the bags slipped sideways. There was a plastic crackle and pop. I ignored it and wept.

It was while I was rubbing salt into the cow that the phone began to ring. I knew who it was so I took my time, put the lid on the casserole and slid it into the preheated oven, then rinsed my hands and dried them before I went to the hall.

I lifted the receiver. 'Hello?'

'Oh, hello. It's Jay Benby from . . .'

I hung up, then stood by the phone and waited.

The phone rang again. I snatched it from the hook.
'Benby,' I spat, 'if you needed to come around here and
rummage through Peter's things all you had to do was
ask. Sending the cops in was completely unnecessary
and heavy-handed. I'm not trying to hide anything from
you and I have no more idea than you where Peter's
money came from. For God's sake, I'd only known him
a few weeks!'

'I'm sorry . . .' Benby's voice was carefully measured.
This was clearly a call he did not want to be making. 'I am
sorry but it was not something I would have done unless I
thought it was necessary. I am not attempting to cast any
sort of aspersions on your character or behaviour, Felicity,
but my professional duties do . . .'

'If you try and justify this I'm going to hang up again. I
don't care about your professional duties – I just want to
know what you are looking for.'

There was a pause. 'Felicity, you are the beneficiary of a large sum. There will be inheritance tax due
on any amount over one hundred and fifty-four thousand pounds and that includes the house and its belongings and any other items of value that may be in the
house. As executor, I am *personally* liable to the Inland
Revenue to ensure all amounts accruing to them are
paid. That is what I mean by professional duties. If you
were the beneficiary *and* the executrix, then I wouldn't
dream of interfering. This matter would be entirely in
your hands.'

I exhaled. I left a long silence. Then I said, slowly and

deliberately, 'What do you mean, any other items of value in the house? What is there?'

Benby paused. 'I have no idea.'

'Bollocks. If you wanted a whole itinerary they would have cleaned the place out, or you would have got bailiffs or something. Don't tell me you were wondering whether his dining-table was an antique. The police went straight to the paperwork.'

'Felicity, please appreciate my position on this. The last thing I want to do is cause any bad feelings between you and myself, I merely want to execute my duties and hand over any monies due to you but I am under an obligation to ensure that all Mr Attwell's assets have been accounted for. I appreciate your annoyance but I really don't think it serves any purpose.'

'Oh Benby,' I sighed. 'What did you expect? Applause?' I hung up.

I returned to the kitchen, where the cow in the oven was beginning to spit and the utensils of my preparations lay scattered panic-stricken across the surfaces. I opened a bottle of red wine and poured some into a glass tumbler. Then I sat at the kitchen table and looked around, calculating how long it would take me to clear up and whether I could sit and think about doing it for long enough to be able to say to myself, by the time I got round to it, *this could have been done by now*.

Executrix. A female executor. Tricksie little things, women.

*

Weekends are the worst for Iris. At least, they feel so. Probably the week is just as bad but then the badness is buried beneath the need to get to work, the scrambling upright, the search for a whole if not clean pair of tights. But Saturdays and Sundays hold very few excuses. It is simply Iris, and the long stretch of time ahead.

She always knows, on the instance of waking, just how bad it is going to be. Very bad, usually. Sometimes she manages to doze, more often she forces herself up, trying to impose a routine on her dull mind and loose, unresponsive body – but that is like trying to carve a sculpture out of jam. Sometimes, while she is half-dressed or eating breakfast, she has a rush of resolution, a sort of internal flurry. She slams down her tea (or muesli, or toast) and runs around throwing things into her handbag while brushing her teeth with the other hand. She is desperate to get out of the flat, convinced that her self-imprisonment there is her only problem and that the minute she is out in the open air she will suddenly feel much, much better.

Storming down the road, towards the shops or the park or the bus-stop, she is overwhelmed with anxiety about whether she should – perhaps – have done her hoovering before she left the house. Wouldn't it be much better to be returning to a clean flat later on when she is tired and wants to sit down with a cup of tea and not think about anything? Sometimes she even pauses in the street, as if she might go back, before remembering that this is one of the sillier tricks her mind occasionally plays. She walks on.

And then, for an hour or two, there is a little peace.

Walking, shopping, going somewhere, these things are like the alcoholic's first few drinks before the bender. It is possible to believe that they are an interlude, not an evasion. It is possible to believe that she is under control.

Later, she becomes tired and realises that her blood sugar has dropped and that this could, if she is not careful, precipitate a panic attack. So she takes sensible, under-control action and goes to a café for tea and cake.

The minute she has sat down and ordered, she knows that it has been a terrible mistake. She doesn't want tea. She wants cake even less. What is she doing wasting time here when every depressive knows that what you should do at the weekends is something constructive? By the time she gets home, the whole afternoon will be gone. Then what? The evening. She can't hoover then. It's much better done in the daylight. She should have gone straight home and had some fruit. Tea is bad for you anyway. Iris is sweating like crazy.

On the table next to her, two women are sitting with two young boys. The mothers are about the same age as Iris, late twenties. They have coffee in white china cups and are trying to ignore their children as much as possible. The boys are nursing lurid pink milkshakes. They have just been to a face-painting class where they have been transformed into tigers. Orange and black stripes decorate their cheeks, their feline features oddly congruous with their tracksuits and trainers. They are hissing at each other across the table and the one nearest to Iris is knocking his leg against her chair, repeatedly. She hates them with a great deal of fierce, lonely venom and wishes she had a twelve-bore shotgun in her handbag.

When her tea arrives, it is unexpectedly pleasant and calms her for a while. The cake appears only a few minutes after her tea is finished, a dark lump of solid sponge punctuated by apple rings and sinking sideways into a puddle of thin, yellowing cream. She eats it quickly but without enthusiasm. As she rises from her table to pay the bill, she can feel it curled up in her stomach like a small but heavy dog.

She is on an even keel. And suddenly, she wishes she could go through the panic again. Anything is better than the weight in her head as she leaves the small, pretty café and begins the slow walk home. Up and down is one thing – productive at least – she often gets a lot of work done during the manic periods and there is always the possibility of variety. But this, this is too formless to be tolerated; this constant, light depression, like a dead dull hand on her dead dull head, like a decomposing crow perched on her shoulder. There is nothing in it that indicates impermanence, no hint that it might ever budge. Perhaps she will spend her whole life in a state of permanent wistfulness, never desperate enough to cry out, never having the energy to fight through the briars or even to ask why. She is too exhausted to even think about it, let alone choose some reasons. Perhaps she is simply mad. Mad without reason. What other kind of madness is there, after all?

*

The cow turned out extremely well, all things considered, emerging a few hours later with a cracked brown crust which oozed delicate little alleyways of warm, honeyed fat. I sliced, experimentally. The flesh inside was stranded brown and pink. I glazed the potatoes with butter and herbs, drained the thin limp fingers of green beans, poured out a dark gravy which dropped softly into the jug, a gleaming drape of satin. I was so pleased with myself that when I heard the doorbell I put on an apron, for effect.

They had bought a bottle of something nice but I was fairly drunk already. I had expected a degree of tension after my phone call with Alex and thought that they probably had too. Consequently, we all relaxed very quickly. As I pulled the plates out of the warmer I found myself thinking, *my friends have come round for dinner*. How nice.

Pudding was cheese and biscuits and fruit and chocolates, which I scattered over Peter's shiny dining-room table – I had been unable to locate a cloth. We picked from one item to the other, leaning back in our chairs and talking about the silly way that our parents' generation had regarded alcohol and drugs and personal debt. Alex had one leg slung over the arm of his chair. He leaned forward and refilled our glasses. I felt warm, friendly and comfortably pissed. I said, 'So why did the police want the paperwork?'

Alex continued to pour wine into my glass, a tiny ruby waterfall which tinkled against the crystal, making the most minute of noises. He spoke without flinching. 'Have you heard of something called bearer shares?'

'Somethings,' said Sophie from the other side of the

table. 'Somethings, strictly speaking. Plural.' I couldn't decide which of us was more drunk.

'Nope,' I said. 'Is that what Peter was into?'

As Alex lifted the bottle away from my glass, he gave it a small turn, so that it would not drip. When he replaced it on the table surface I waited for the clunking sound as the glass met the polished wood. It never came. 'That,' said Alex, leaning back in his seat, 'is what all three of us were into, in a way.'

'Is it illegal?'

Alex laughed. 'If it was you'd have to arrest half of the City of London and a lot others besides. No, it's not illegal. Although some people use it because they don't have to register ownership of a company so it's open to abuse, I suppose, but basically it means what it says. Bearer shares. Whoever bears the shares has got the company. Finders keepers.'

'What company?'

It was Alex's first tell-tale pause. 'The company that the three of us set up together. Import and export.'

I took a sip of my wine and frowned. 'How does Benby know about this?'

'He probably doesn't, probably just guessing. Peter might have mentioned a holding or something like that. The point is that he has a legal obligation to find out, that's why he's so jumpy. Strictly speaking, he could have you evicted from here, you know, although he'd be bonkers to do it. You could sue him for being a bad executor. He's in a very tricky position.'

I sat up and banged my glass down indignantly. A little of the wine slopped onto the shiny table and lay in a perfect, unabsorbed pool. 'But it's my house!'

'You've still got to pay tax on it.'

I sat back again. Who would have thought that being in an unexpected drama like this could be so complex, so full of mundane detail? All these minutiae were interfering with my trauma.

'Which brings me to the main point . . .' Alex glanced over at Sophie, then back at me.

'Go on,' I said.

'Strictly speaking, Peter's third of the company belongs to you. But it's worthless. Sophie and I have a controlling share and can wind the whole thing up. Add its assets and it's debts together and you come up with zero. Having said that, if your solicitor and the Inland Revenue get involved it all get's rather sticky and uncomfortable for us. The taxman thinks that forty per cent of your third is his and might not quite understand why it comes out at nothing. The bearer shares are worthless to you, they just mean a lot of complications and could possibly delay you sorting things out on the house and so on. However, they are not worthless to us. We would like to keep things going.'

'If you have them does that mean Benby is off my back?'

Alex spread his hands. 'It means there is nothing for him to find. He can send the bailiffs in if he wants. There'll be nothing. He can make his executor's oath with a clear conscience, hand over your slice, give the tax man his and everybody's happy.'

I had put some music on in the background, Spanish guitar from Peter's collection. It chose this point to conclude. There was a brief, eerie pause as we all registered the silence.

'You don't have to do it,' Sophie's voice was soft. 'We're not putting any pressure on you. You might not want to take our word for it.'

I looked from one to the other. The house we were sitting in was worth, I reckoned, around three hundred thousand pounds. Peter had had twenty grand in various accounts and life insurance which would give around fifty. Then there were the household goods, a few bonds and shares and, to cap it all, an allotment somewhere and a boat moored in Suffolk. I was, as Benby would have said, a *wealthy woman*. I was also a woman with a great deal of paperwork to do.

I hardly knew Alex and Sophie. I liked them, but that meant nothing. It was possible that they were lying to me and that a third of their company was worth a very great deal, but somehow I doubted it. They didn't seem rich to me, just plump and self-satisfied. And anyway, after the Inland Revenue had been in, my third would be just over a sixth.

All at once, I was overcome with a wave of exhaustion, a tearful longing for someone, anyone, to gather me up and decide all the things that were there to be decided. Sophie, Alex, Benby, the police; if the window-cleaner had stepped into the room that minute and offered to sort everything out I probably would have given the entire legacy to him.

'Where do you think they are?' I asked.

Sophie smiled. She knew they were home and dry. Alex was not so sure. 'Definitely nothing in the study?' he asked.

I shook my head. 'The police didn't get anything. If I had come across anything I didn't understand I would have pulled it out.'

Alex made a face. 'No idea then. Probably the best thing would be if we came over one weekend and went through the whole place, all three of us.'

'Couldn't they be somewhere else?' I asked. 'A bank or something.'

Both Alex and Sophie laughed. 'Not Peter,' Sophie said. 'They'll be here all right. Peter liked to gather all the things he needed under his roof, where he could keep an eye on them.'

There was a pause.

I stood, unsteadily, and managed to say, 'Coffee,' before turning away to the kitchen.

Once there, I huddled against a wall with my arms pulled up over my chest and my fists against my face. It is a stance I adopt when I am worried and trying to work something out, a self-protective stance – the upright version of the foetal position.

The wine was swimming in my head. The wall behind me felt pliant. On the counter opposite, the ruined remnants of the joint sat cooling in the roasting dish, the golden-orange fat solidifying into something thick and white and unpleasant.

All the things he needed, under his roof.

I felt very lonely, and cold.

3

*I*ris arrives for work at ten-thirty each morning. She is later than most people who work in the building because she gets the first off-peak train, after nine-thirty, which is cheaper. It means that she often stays later than everybody else as well, but she would probably do that anyway. There isn't much to go home for, after all.

Most mornings, she is greeted by Tomlinson. Tomlinson is the porter, a small man who rarely smiles but manages to exude an air of weary benevolence, nonetheless. His rotting old building is one of the cheapest in central London and he knows it. As a result, he has seen a lot of firms come and go, one-person set-ups like Iris's, the occasional charity. Once in a while, the management get in some tenant of whom he disapproves, which is the only time he comes to life and gossips. There were some girls in the office below Iris, he told her once, who sold items of clothing made of rubber. He told her this with such solemnity she found it hard not to burst out laughing.

He is supposed to work normal office hours but often seems to be around in the evenings. Tenants have keys to let themselves in the back door if they want to use their offices at weekends. He is so much a part of the building that Iris finds it hard to believe that he also has a home to go to at night. She has a mental picture of him in a cubbyhole somewhere in the basement, with an old pallet bed surrounded by a curtain and a single gas ring, perhaps keeping bottles of milk on the windowsill. She hasn't a clue where he really lives and he knows nothing about her either. Their conversations have never ventured that far.

His office is to the left of the entrance, although office is a rather grand word for the tiny room where he sits during working hours, glancing out of the door at anyone who comes through the main entrance, giving them a cursory nod if he knows them and ignoring them if he doesn't. Somewhere on her lease agreement, he is referred to as *security*, which means – as far as Iris can tell – that if he doesn't like the look of somebody entering the building he will do up the buttons on his jacket before ignoring them. The portering went out to tender the previous month and for a while it looked as though they were going to get some flash security guard, a young man on one pound fifty an hour who had probably been turned down by the police because he was too butch and too surly even for them. When a note arrived from the leaseholding company to the effect that the portering services would remain unchanged, Iris had felt a flush of relief. It was hard to imagine what sort of person would manage to undercut Tomlinson.

Postal deliveries are left in a set of wooden pigeonholes next to Tomlinson's office. Iris's pigeonhole is marked with her room number, 314. Most of the other holes are empty. As she removes the envelopes, Tomlinson sticks his head out of his office and nods at her. He is eating and has biscuit crumbs stuck to his lower lip, although he usually has crumbs on his lip whether he is eating or not. He is pointing at a small stack of cardboard boxes next to the pigeonholes.

'Them yours?' he asks.

She bends and peers at the address: *The Popular Paper Company.* Popular Paper were a bunch of lads in open-necked shirts who spent three months on the first floor trying to set up some sort of stationery business. Then they did a runner, still owing the rent for the entire period of their tenancy. Their pigeonhole is crammed full of items of post, some of which have red lettering just visible through the paper windows in the envelopes. Once, Iris walked past their office on her way out and found two burly men banging on it, their faces set.

'No,' says Iris. 'It's Popular Paper again.'

Tomlinson bends and peers down at the boxes. 'Not with me it ain't,' he mutters as he straightens, turning back to his office.

In the lift up to the third floor, Iris flicks through her post, in the hope of seeing a postmark she doesn't recognise or an unfamiliar hand. Today, there is a large white envelope with a card in it. She opens it, holding the rest of the letters against her chest with her upper arm. *LADIES!* says the front of the card in elegant capitals, above a picture of a young woman wearing a white blouse. The woman has her back to the camera and her hands on her hips, she is looking over her shoulder and smiling. Long dark hair snakes immaculately over billowing silk. The cuffs of the blouse go almost up to the elbow and are fastened by rows of tiny buttons. The woman's smile is slightly stiff, as though the position is a little uncomfy and the photographer has asked her to hold it a fraction too long. Inside the card is *a personal invitation* to her, *Iris Farrow*, to a private view of exclusive blouses exclusively for *executive women* such as herself. A complimentary glass of white wine will be served. Iris puts the card back in the envelope. Somehow, somewhere, she has been put onto a database of women who have their own businesses or work in management. Every now and then she gets letters wanting to know if her fleet of company cars would benefit from a special maintenance deal or whether all of her employees have pension schemes.

As she makes her way down the tattered carpet that leads to her office she wonders who is more deluded, them or her. She always comes to work in a skirt and jacket, even if she has no appointments. She knows some self-employed people who rent desks in open-plan units so that telephone callers will hear a lot of background noise and imagine them to have a fully-staffed office at their beck and call. Getting potential customers to take you seriously is no problem as long as you can convince yourself.

Late-twentieth-century woman, thinks Iris, as she rattles her key in the lock; self-sufficient, in complete control of her delusions. We have won the right to be alone but that was only half the battle – now we have to win the right not to need to be alone to get anywhere. Her door needs servicing. To admit herself, she has to insert the key, twist, pull it out a fraction, then twist again. Her kettle is broken too.

Her office is painted white. The filing cabinet is dark green metal. The grey hulk of her PC sits waiting on her desk, underneath its cream-coloured plastic cover with the dark red trim. The answer-phone/fax has spewed out a stream of paper which has spilled over the desk in thin folds. She goes over and rips it clear, then tosses it onto the desk without looking at it.

Outside, a tiny, sick, yellow glint of sun is struggling through the thick white cloud. It clearly will not last.

*

The thing about promiscuity is, you can't expect them to keep ringing you up and asking to see you again. If they do that, you aren't being promiscuous. *That*, my dears, is called serial monogamy, which is just about as radical or enjoyable as playing badminton each Wednesday. To be promiscuous, you have to keep it short and snappy.

Bill was short and snappy. Especially snappy. That man was pure testosterone.

A typical night with Bill involved him coming round to my place, sex, a trip to the pub then to an Indian restaurant, then back to my place for more sex. In the morning, before breakfast, lunch or dinner and just for a change, we would have sex. Bill was shameless, and somehow his shamelessness transmitted itself to me, as if he had passed on a sexual disease – which, in a way, I suppose he had. I went into that relationship still willing to conform, to moan about afterplay, to discuss my finer feelings. I emerged from it dry-eyed. I don't think there was ever a point when I realised that sex didn't matter any more, that the more enjoyable it was the less it mattered. The knowledge seeped into me via . . . well you can guess where, like a form of osmosis. The seed was planted and the idea took route. I can screw who I like now, I thought.

If Bill was short then so was the relationship, so talk of a typical night is, perhaps, a little over-flattering to both of us. I think it was the third or fourth time we went out that he leaned over the table in the Taj Mahal, picked up the mango chutney and said, 'There's a new assistant on the floor below me and she's got great legs. Married though, I think.'

In a millisecond, I comprehended: *Bill is mentioning another woman in terms of being sexually attracted to her which means that subconsciously he is trying to tell me that what we have is just sex; this is something of a blow to my ego because I find it utterly unreasonable that any man should not fall hysterically in love with me; however if he was hysterically in love with me I would be completely horrified because he's shorter than me and not a very nice person; still it's been worth it because he's great in the sack and it's always worthwhile expanding oneself, let's face it; and it would be very immature and unintelligent of me to get in a huff when all he is telling me is that this is as insignificant to him as it is to me.*

'Oh,' I said, cracking a poppadom, 'I wouldn't let that stop you.'

In the morning, he trotted back from the toilet wagging an enormous erection, which I could not fail to miss as I rolled over because it almost hit me in the eye. He had clambered onto the bed and was now kneeling over me, whereupon he proceeded to tap me on the head. 'Wakey wakey,' he said cheerfully, the erection thumping softly in my hair. 'Time to come out and play.'

I rolled away, groaning, and regarded him; the proudly rounded belly, the solid arms, the gentle hang of flesh beneath the chin. This was a man who would snarl like fury if *I* woke *him* up a clear hour before we had agreed, and there he was, kneeling above me, displaying himself with the kind of self-regard which women have knocked out of them by the age of six. He was five foot seven, a whole stone overweight and had fair hair that looked limp and greasy ten minutes after he had washed it. But he was sexy as fuck and he knew it – and because he knew it, that made him sexy; the chicken and the egg.

Which came first, I wondered, the confidence or the prowess? Perhaps somewhere there was a woman intimidated enough by her own deficiencies to praise him at the stage he needed it most. Now he had it. He didn't even know he had it but he did know that it worked.

He looked down and regarded his true love, the stalwart little friend who still stood – stalwartly – refusing to let him down. He reached down and fiddled with it, pulling back the foreskin and brushing at the shiny head, as if there might be a bit of fluff or something on it. Then he looked at me and asked contemplatively, 'Don't you wish you had one of these?'

I raised an eyebrow and drawled, '*Darling*, with what I've got, I can have one of *those* any time I like.'

I was learning fast.

After Bill, there was no stopping me. A typical week in the life of a promiscuous woman might go thus:

Monday. Do something foolish with a married man called Paul who pays for dinner and commits the gross error of telling me, with an earnest expression on his face, that I am worth every penny. A row ensues, which means that both of us know it is over before it's begun.

Tuesday. Mid-morning, ring Paul's answer-machine. It tells me how sorry he is that he is not available. I say, 'Paul, sweetie-pie, the flowers are absolutely beautiful but totally unnecessary. I presume they're from you anyway, no note. I wasn't offended in the slightest. I thought the whole thing was ever so funny, actually. Thanks.'

Wednesday. The reappearance of John, an age-old fling who belches with gusto. I try to work out why I find it so offensive and conclude this: farting smells worse, but I am not in the habit of kissing men on the bum.

Thursday. A work colleague comes over for dinner. We eat a mountain of spaghetti, snow-capped by carbonara, and then he rolls a joint. The atmosphere is awkward.

Earlier, I have joked that he may not stay the night. He has joked in return that he doesn't want to, which we both know is untrue. Now we are drunk and I feel a little guilty. I know I am about to insist he sticks around and he will respond by insisting he should leave; both of us arguing, with some vigour, the merits of the opposite to what we want.

Friday. It is time for some serious sex. John doesn't count. Neither does the work colleague (who got his way in the end and must now be handled carefully in case he tells). At a jazz café in EC1, I pick up a blond stranger called Halvard who tells me that neither of his parents was Norwegian. I have both hands on his buttocks at the time and he has his left hand on my left breast. His parentage is not what is uppermost in my mind – but it is clearly something he wants to get out in the open before we go any further. I have drunk so much that I am almost sober. We are in the corridor leading to the toilets and every now and then a door bangs and someone emerges. The women glance our way and strut by with a superior air. The men do up their flies and sneak envious looks at my chest. One claps Halvard, chummily, on the back.

I plaster my lips to his and our tongues slither together with all the finesse of a pair of sprats squirming around the bottom of a fishing vessel. I push back and say, 'Let's get out of here.'

Back at my place, there is some pretence of making tea. While I fill the kettle, Halvard struggles to open a bottle of wine, which annoys me because I know we won't drink it and it's a bottle wasted. He is leaning against the kitchen table with his hip and swearing softly in a language which I can't identify. When he finally gets the cork out, he plonks the bottle down on the table with a triumphant shout that sounds like *hurrah* with lots of extra consonants. I get a sudden image of him bringing down a moose. When I turn round he is watching me, smiling idiotically.

'No milk,' I slur, as I plonk my arms onto his shoulders, one by one, *plonk, plonk*. 'No milk.' As we tumble inexpertly towards the bedroom it occurs to me that if we are too pissed to make a cup of tea there is no guarantee that we are sober enough to have decent sex.

Well, who said it had to be decent?

Saturday. After Halvard has gone I bathe and pull on a crisp, clean t-shirt and newly washed jeans. I enjoy the slight abrasion of the denim as I work the jeans up over my legs, the tightness around my thighs and crotch, the feeling that I am fresh and corseted.

I have managed to drink some black tea but muesli without milk is out of the question. I tried it with water once. It looked like something I had vomited. So, I pull another cardigan on top of the one I am already wearing and slope off to the corner shop, keys and purse in hand.

On my way back, something happens that stays with me for days. I am walking up the hill, along a wide pavement with a grass verge between it and the road. It is windy and I have my head down. I glance up to see that at the top of the hill is a drunk, standing by the edge of the path, feet in the verge, motionless but for a barely perceptible sway. Both his arms are by his sides and he is holding a can of beer in one hand and a stone in the other. His head is hanging as if it is slightly disconnected from his neck, like the nodding dogs you used to see in the back of cars, except his head is not nodding. From where I am I can just make out the look on his dirty, matted face. It is one of pure malice. It is the look of a man who is lonely and miserable and angry and ready to take out his anger on anyone more fortunate than himself. Women are always prime targets for these men, much more so than other men. Women, they believe, have no idea how hard life is, because the women who end up on the streets don't seem like women at all.

I am walking towards him and I am a woman cradling a large sliced loaf, a carton of orange juice, a pint of milk, a packet of bacon and some lavatory-cleaner. My purse is firmly visible in my grasp. The keys to my warm, cosy flat dangle invitingly from my plastic fish keyring which is looped over one finger. To him, I must look like somebody well worth hating.

I move out into the road as if I am going to cross it and walk up it slowly, acting as though I have not noticed him while keeping a careful eye. It is a quiet street and no-one else is around. I have snapped into the mode of thinking that I always use after dark, anywhere: stay casual but alert, note the nearest front door to bang on if necessary, walk in a manner which is confident but not confrontational. Don't, whatever you do, act like a victim.

Then, behind me and to the left, I hear a noise, the squeaking of wheels. I turn to see that a girl of about eight is cycling up the path, her bike wobbling and her breathing audible from effort. She is cycling towards the drunk, who has now begun to lift the can of beer towards his face.

I watch, horrified, rigid with fear for the girl. She hasn't even noticed him. She continues to peddle slowly. When she reaches him, she passes without so much as a sideways glance. I am breathless at her audacity.

When I draw level with the drunk, I pluck up the courage to glance over at his face. He has lowered his beer and is standing in the same position as before, motionless. His gaze is still, his eyes glassy. He is clearly in no position to notice me or anybody. I clutch my breakfast to my chest and as I turn the corner into my own street I am thinking, was I really that fearless at her age? At what point in my life did I unlearn courage – and how come I didn't notice it happening?

It's obvious, I suppose. I didn't notice it because I was too busy noticing other things: that drunks can be dangerous, sometimes; that how you walk makes a difference; that you must never forget for one minute how many reasons there are for a man – any man – to hate you.

*

Half past six at night. Hometime. Iris corrects herself. Time to leave. Even though she is still in the office, pushing her chair back, standing, she knows that by the time she gets home it will be one of those nights when she can't be bothered to cook. She often can't be bothered with food, which bothers her. There are many things about her life which she regards as strong and singular and worthy but there is something about the rituals surrounding food – from supermarket shelf to drying up the dishes – which fills her with despair. She simply cannot bring herself to cook a decent dinner. It would be too poignant for words.

So, tonight, there is the usual choice: a takeaway, some dried pasta, or a potato microwaved beyond recognition so that its skin is clammy and its insides mutated into the approximate consistency of soap.

She bends forward and depresses the button on the back of her PC, which makes a small, piteous whining noise as the power dies.

Her phone rings. She picks it up and says brightly, 'Hello? Iris Farrow?' There is no reply. From the acoustic on the line, it sounds as though the caller has not connected properly. She repeats, 'Hello?' Nothing. She hangs up.

As she is pulling on her coat, the phone rings again. This time, she hesitates before deciding to let the answer-phone get it. She waits by her desk. Distorted only slightly by the machine, a familiar voice spills into the room. 'Iris, it's George; listen I refuse to believe you've left this early, you sad old workaholic, so if you're in the loo or something then ring . . .' She picks up the phone and George continues as if he doesn't know it is the real Iris he is now addressing as opposed to Iris the machine. ' . . . me when you get back or you can ring me tomorrow and leave a message on my machine and then I can programme it to ring yours. Do you know what I've got now? Voice mail. Stick that in your pipe and smoke it you old IBMer, you little technophobe . . .'

'George,' sighs Iris. 'What are you talking about?'

'Voice mail,' says George. 'It's taking over the world. Nearly everybody has it now, well all the big companies anyway, and seeing as I'm going to be massive one day I thought I'd jump in ahead of the game. Do you know, I can now programme my machine to ring yours and leave a message when I am out and so are you? If you had voice mail too then we'd never need to talk to each other.' George breaks into song. 'Let your mach-ine, do the talking.' He stops singing. 'I tell you kiddo, this is going to make human beings redundant.'

'They said that about the wheel.'

'And they were right. When was the last time you hailed a human in the street and asked it to take you to Liverpool Street?'

'George, as you said, I'm a sad workaholic and at the moment I'm a tired, hungry sad workaholic so what do you want?'

'Oh you know, a little human contact . . .' Iris waits patiently, smiling in spite of herself. George Leary gets up her nose on a regular basis but she finds him impossible to resent. 'Human contact *and* . . . a loan of your Global Scan manual. For a couple of days. You get it back by Friday and if you're really lucky I buy lunch and tell you about voice mail in comprehensive detail.'

'You've missed your vocation and if I don't go now I'll miss my train.'

'Get the next one. I'll meet you in the Cittie of Yorke in twenty minutes. You'll recognise me: I'm the one in the cheeky grin – I'll recognise you because you'll have a big fat book under your arm.'

'Two days?'

'Back by Friday.'

'I want gin, not lager. And by the way if your new voice box thing is so great how come it can't put you through first time round?'

'What?'

'Didn't you ring a minute ago?'

'Not me.'

When their call is finished, Iris replaces the receiver with a small smile. She likes George and he makes no attempt to hide the fact that he likes her. He has an office similar to hers, in Boot Lane, where he works with a partner and a part-time assistant who answers the phone squeaking, 'George-Leary-Associates-how-may-I-help-you-hello?' Occasionally, Iris and George do some work together. About once every three months, he makes a pass at her and it is a cause of some regret to both of them that, chummy as they are, Iris cannot bring herself to fancy him. George has a beaked nose and a growing bald patch, along with a slight droop to the right hand corner of his mouth which means that when he talks he looks as though he is chewing a toffee at the same time. The fact is, there is not the remotest chance of Iris ever sleeping with him unless he is prepared to have major reconstructive surgery.

Even so, she feels a little lighter as she pulls out the manual from the stack that is piled high on the floor next to her desk. A drink after work. What could be more civilised, more normal?

Locking her office door behind her as she leaves, she hears movement at the end of the corridor and turns in time to see a figure slipping round the corner. Tomlinson. She was planning to speak to him on the way out. Her heater is still not working properly.

'Mr Tomlinson!' she calls out. She pauses. 'Hello?'

Her voice echoes down the corridor where it stretches into darkness. Various other corridors and office doors lead off it and at the end she can just see the shadow of the back stairwell. She never uses the back stairs. The lift is near her end of the building. She frowns to herself. Tomlinson could not be hiding in a doorway and wouldn't have had time to reach the end of the corridor. If he had let himself into one of the other offices she would have heard the rattle of his keys. Perhaps he is not in the mood for requests. She will have to catch him in the morning.

As she emerges from the lift on the ground floor, she glances over to Tomlinson's room and sees that his door is ajar and he is moving around inside. For him to have reached his room in the time it took her to descend in the lift would have meant him sprinting from the top floor. Tomlinson doesn't look as if he could sprint to save his life. She hesitates and with that hesitation becomes less certain that there was somebody in the corridor after all, then certain again, all within the space of a second. It could well have been another tenant, lost or just exploring – she has often been intrigued by the building's history and meant to have a look around. Victorian, she thinks. A thief? Her office door has two locks. She always puts the Chubb on at the end of the day. If the worst comes to the worst she's insured. Suppose there was a small-time crook lurking on the third floor? Suppose she asked Tomlinson to investigate and he went up there and got his head caved in by some desperate adolescent who was only after a few handbags and never meant to kill but was surprised and frightened? She would find the body in the morning. She would have to give evidence in court.

Iris shakes her head and decides that what she needs most is a drink.

In the Cittie of Yorke, George is waiting in a wooden snug with a pint of lager, a large gin and tonic for her and two packets of cream cheese and chive flavoured crisps. The minute he sees her, he rips open both packets and takes a crisp from each.

'What took you?' he warbles with his mouth full, 'and where the hell's the manual?'

Iris sinks down opposite him and slaps her forehead. 'George I'm such an idiot, do you want me to go back and get it?'

George seems unbothered. 'Nah. Who wants to talk shop? Let's just gossip.'

For ten minutes or so, they do. There is an information

technology conference coming up in a couple of months which will be attended by several hundred people like themselves. George's theory is that small businesspeople always go wild at conferences because they are so relieved to have colleagues for a couple of days. Last year, two hundred of them went to an Elizabethan banquet where a King and Queen sat on a raised podium at the end of long trestle tables waving chicken drumsticks and a jester gambolled up and down jangling bells in people's ears while they were trying to eat. Every time you wanted more mead you had to stand up, wave both arms in the air and shout, 'Yo, Wench!', upon which a woman in a frilly apron would come and pour it from an earthenware jug. George said it was the worst wine he had ever tasted. It was so bad that he sank great quantities of it and later led their table in a dance – that old Elizabethan favourite, the Conga.

This year, there is talk of a mixed sauna. The very thought makes Iris's hair stand on end: two hundred semi-naked information technologists.

'Still,' George is saying, 'there'll be no misbehaving for me this year.' Last year, George was caught groping a business librarian from Woolwich behind a cigarette machine. One of the wenches came across them when she went to refill her earthenware jug and returned to announce her discovery to the entire table. They received a round of applause when they returned, from all but the business librarian's boyfriend who sat staring glumly ahead until the court jester came along and pulled six tiny red sponge balls from his left ear, which seemed to cheer him up no end.

'I'm in love,' George says abruptly.

'Oh?' At first, Iris thinks he is joking. Whatever George has got up to at conferences, he has always made a point of telling her, a week or so later, that the only reason he ever tries anything on with any other woman is because she has broken his heart.

George's voice has become very still and even. 'Her name is Jerry. And she's beautiful.'

Iris pauses for a moment, absorbing both the information and the tone of voice in which it is being delivered. Then she feels a sudden flush of jealousy. She does not want George but has got used to being wanted by him.

She asks a few innocuous-sounding questions. How old is she? What does she do? She is hoping that one of his answers will render this Jerry person unsuitable but George gives all the right answers. Jerry is twenty-four, six years younger than him. She is a secretary for the Financial Research Consultancy down the corridor. He got to know her because his company and hers have some reciprocal arrangement whereby he lets them use his e-mail in return for access to their colour photocopier.

'Amazing isn't it,' he says. 'Love. I don't quite believe it myself – but now I need the loo.'

While he is in the toilet, Iris starts to feel annoyed. This little drink-after-work turns out to have an ulterior motive. He did not want to borrow her manual or talk about his new voice mail system. He wanted to tell her about Jerry. It was probably subconscious. He probably believed his excuses to be genuine – but that somehow made it all the worse.

When George returns from the toilet he plonks himself down on her side of the table, on the wooden bench, and slides up to her, pressing flirtatiously against her shoulder. Two weeks ago, he would have never dared to be so physical but now he is too flush with his own happiness to care how she reacts.

'Enough about me,' he says. 'I want to talk about you.'

She looks at him. He means it. 'Look,' he says, casting his gaze down at the table, as if unwrapping the challenge. 'I'm not going to get all heavy or anything. I just want to know how you are these days. I know you're strolling around as if everything is fine and I know how easy it is to get into the habit of that. Believe me, I know. And I'm just saying this is your opportunity to tell me that actually, no, everything is not fine and you're still really chewed up about that bastard.' He stops, sensing that she has stiffened in her seat. He looks at her. 'You can talk to me,' he adds.

Iris is thinking, so, there *was* an ulterior motive – just not the one that I thought. She can feel that her face is rigid with dismay.

'Oh come on,' he says. 'Let me get you another.' He reaches for her glass.

She puts a hand out to prevent him. 'George,' she says, her voice light and cool, 'sweet as this is, do not imagine that just because you've got the hots for some secretary down the corridor you suddenly know all there is to know about love and human relationships. You don't know me nearly as well as you think.'

By the look on his face, she can tell that she has hurt

his feelings badly. He picks up their glasses and mutters, 'Sorry ... well ... let's have another anyway.'

He rises and turns towards the bar, even though the last thing that either of them wants now is another drink. Conversation will be stilted. A small seed of resentment has been planted which may yet grow fertile fruit. Iris watches him as he shoulders his way through the early-evening crowd of City boys. Even from behind, he looks defeated. Her remark has brought him back down to earth, reminded him of a few small cold realities – like the one about how difficult it is to get to know somebody when you fancy them, how easy it is to make mistakes. We all get our knickers in a twist sometimes, she thinks with miserable pride, why should he be any different, just because he's nicer than most people? Which of us, after all, can tell the difference between effortless charm and effortless duplicity?

The next thing she knows, she is leaning back against the wall of the snug and George has one hand on her shoulder. He is saying her name but his voice sounds as if it is coming from far away. Then it swoops towards her and booms in her ear. She jerks upright, as though she has been having a nightmare, even though she has not been asleep.

Over George's shoulder looms a face, a plump face with a lipless mouth which moves and says, 'Do you need a hand mate?'

George is talking over his shoulder. 'No, I think she's all right now. Thanks.'

Iris feels clammy. She pushes George away and says, 'What?'

George moves back to give her some air. 'Iris,' he says, 'what's going on?'

'Nothing.' She is bewildered.

'I came back from the bar and you looked as though you had fainted or gone into a trance or something, but your eyes were open. What happened?'

Iris can feel tears of panic welling up, her throat is rough and dry. 'Nothing . . . nothing . . . I don't remember . . .'

George takes her hands in his. 'Okay . . .okay . . . it's all right. Just sit here for a bit. Do you want me to get you some water or something?'

Iris shakes her head, unable to speak.

George's expression suddenly changes. 'Oh God Iris, don't tell me the helicopter pilot got you pregnant.'

'No . . .' Iris mutters thickly, 'I'm not bloody pregnant, not unless it's the next immaculate conception anyway. A blue dress. I saw a blue dress.'

'Beth?' says George.

She frowns at him, still shaking her head. What the hell is he talking about?

'That was what you said as I put my hand on your shoulder,' George says. 'I think that's what it was. I couldn't hear. You were mumbling.'

Tears slide down Iris's face, although the panic has begun to subside. She withdraws her hands from George's and fumbles in her sleeve for a tissue. 'I don't know,' she says, thinly. 'I don't know what happened. One minute you

66

were on the way to the bar and then you were back here but I didn't black out or anything. I don't know what it was. And I don't know anyone called Beth.'

George says nothing. He sits and looks at her, and his face which is usually so odd and jokey is suddenly plain with concern. All she can do is shake her head, shrug slightly, and shake her head again. But a voice inside her is whispering, *you were right all along. And this is just the beginning*.

4

Time was short. I realised that as I waved Sophie and Alex goodbye from Peter's front doorstep. They wanted to come over and go through the house with me the following weekend. I had four days. That was presuming that Benby was not about to send in the big boys. Four days, and no idea where to start.

In the end, it was started for me. The phone rang as I was sipping coffee in the kitchen the following morning, trying to be gentle with myself because my head hurt like hell. I half expected it to be Benby threatening bailiffs so my voice must have sounded wary as I answered, 'Hello?'

'Oh. Hello.' The voice on the other end was a woman's voice, accent uncertain and sounding slightly surprised, as if she wasn't expecting anybody to answer. I waited.

'Is that Beth?' the woman asked.

'Er, it's Bet actually. Yes.'

'Oh I'm sorry. Bet.' She pronounced it hesitantly, as if the word was in a foreign language. 'Bet. You won't remember, but we met really quickly at the crematorium. We didn't really get introduced. You left. Somebody told me your name was Beth.'

I had come downstairs without my slippers on. There was no carpet in the hall, just dark parquet flooring polished to an unnatural glow. I was standing pigeon-toed and had my left foot crossed over my right to keep it warm. I looked down at my bare ankles and remembered the woman's hand gripping my sleeve, her long nails denting my black jacket. I remembered that despite her immaculate appearance she had seemed a little uncontrolled – if it is possible to be only a little uncontrolled, that is. Her appearance in the supermarket had been startling by contrast; rushed, dowdy, unkempt. At Peter's funeral she had seemed like a woman with an image which was about to crack into a thousand tiny fissures, like a shattering windscreen. Hurrying away from me in Sainsbury's she was more like a person with no image at all; the kind of woman you see in shops every day, blurred by the hectic business of childrearing and its attendant difficulties. The woman in the supermarket would have had a great deal of gathering to do before there was anything to shatter.

I crossed my feet, right onto left, rubbing. 'Yes,' I said. 'I had to go, that's right.' I knew, somehow, that the glimpse we had had of each other out shopping was not going to be mentioned, not over the phone anyway.

'How are you?' she blurted suddenly; a question she had to get out of the way before she could ask what she really wanted.

I didn't know how to respond. 'Well. I'm OK. I've

got quite a lot of sorting out to do, the house and so on.'

'The house?' The register of her voice shot up by an octave. She was almost squeaking. 'Oh yes,' she came back down. 'Yes of course.'

I was not prepared to keep the small talk going, although it might have put her more at her ease. My coffee was cooling in the kitchen and my feet were going purple; and I had resolved, after last night's dinner, that if anybody else wanted anything out of me they were going to have to ask outright. I was losing patience with all these hidden agendas.

'Are you very busy then?' she said, continuing straight on without giving me time to answer. 'Because, I'm sure you are. But I wondered if we could get together. I wanted to have a chat with you, about him, if that's OK. It's none of my business I know but I thought you might find it useful.'

That last bit was pure bullshit. But by now I was starting to feel sorry for her. Whatever her agenda might be, she was clearly going to be rather bad at hiding it. After Benby's smooth hypocrisy and the casual manipulations of Alex and Sophie I felt quite intrigued by the thought of talking to somebody who was clearly in an even bigger mess than I was. 'Yes. Fine, no problem. Do you want to come over?'

'No,' she answered quickly. 'No I don't want to come to the house if you don't mind. That's if . . . I'd just prefer not to, that's all. I wondered if you'd come over here, I live in Burnt Oak. It's just I've got the little one, my boy. I don't have anyone to look after him at the moment and it's a bit difficult to get out. If you came over here I can give him something to play with or if you can make it just after lunch then he'll be having his nap. It's much easier then. Not running around, you know.'

'Yes . . .' I said chummily, although I hadn't the faintest idea what life must be like with a toddler and no desire to find out. 'Yes of course, when . . .'

'Today?'

After the phone call was finished, I padded back to the kitchen. My coffee was lukewarm and my toes numb but I felt cheered and invigorated. I was going to discover something that other people didn't want me to know. I threw back the lid of the stainless steel bread-bin and it made a satisfying clang. There were the remnants of a loaf flopping in an open plastic bag. I rummaged for a couple of slices and dropped them into the toaster, then, with the other hand, flicked the switch on the electric kettle, so that I could water down and warm up my coffee. I had said I would be there around two, which gave me the whole of the morning to begin a proper search of the house. I would do the garage. It would be one complete thing out of the way – and best to do it in daylight.

I leaned my elbows on the edge of the sink and gazed out at the garden while I waited for my toast to pop. Beneath the window was a cool flood of dark green grass which swooped down to a rockery, now slightly overgrown. The garden was encircled by a tall, rich privet hedge which concealed it from the view of neighbouring houses, although their top floors and roofs could be seen; the occasional dormer window. It was a wealthy but tasteless neighbourhood: new houses, all clean and antiseptic; recent, respectable money from good salaries and golden handshakes – the kind of area where nobody would imagine anything about anybody else. Great cover. Ideal, in fact.

There was a sudden flurry of brown as a thrush came to rest on the windowsill. Its wings clattered briefly against the glass as it shook itself then froze, its tiny eye fixed upon me, waiting for me to move. I stood up slowly so as not to frighten it. 'One thing,' the woman had said as our phone call had concluded. 'Just one thing, I hope you don't mind. I really don't want you to mention this to the Littletons.'

It had taken me a moment or two to realise who she was talking about.

'The Littletons,' she had said. 'We don't get on, really. I'll explain in more detail, well, later. But actually, it's quite important. Look, just please don't mention this to them.'

Alex and Sophie. Sophie and Alex. Mr and Mrs Littleton, who thought they had me all sewn up.

The toaster made a small mechanical clang and the two slices of toast jumped a clear inch upwards then dropped back down, scattering crumbs. When I glanced back at the window I saw that the thrush had taken fright and was gone.

Burnt Oak is the last stop before Edgware, which is a

peculiarly damning indictment, if you ask me. What is more depressing than being the penultimate, the number two, the runner-up? People who live in Burnt Oak do not even have the perverse glamour of inner-city deprivation. There are no riots in Burnt Oak, just the occasional fracas at a bus-stop. The residents probably don't commit suicide much, as a rule, unless they allow themselves to die from boredom. They are not on the edge, after all – just near it.

The Mini wouldn't start, so I had to get the train, which was probably what put me in such a bad mood. When I got there, I stood in the station ticket hall, making a confused and desultory scan of the Local Area map. (Those things always drive me mad because I can never work out whether I am upside-down or not.) Then I went out of the station and hovered, glancing left and right, trying to get my bearings.

The station was in the middle of a row of run-down shops: a launderette with flock wallpaper and a peeling exterior; a school and sportswear shop of the kind you don't think exists anymore; windows full of child-sized, blank-faced dummies in navy duffel-coats, their limbs twisted in palsied attitudes. An elderly man in a motorised wheelchair droned anxiously by. Two teenage boys sat on their heels, staring while they smoked. Ye Gods, I thought glumly, I wouldn't last ten minutes round here.

I had checked my *A-Z* before I left home but forgotten to bring it with me. Left out of the station, I seemed to remember – providing I was right way up – and past a church, which turned out to be huge, red-brick and evangelical.

Beyond the shops were row after row of job-lot, pebble-dash housing. I was in the dead zone.

Her house was in the middle of it, approximately twenty minutes from the station. In front of her row was an unfenced rectangle of green grass enlivened only by a council sign which said NO BALL GAMES. To ring the bell, I had to step inside a porch with wavery glass panels and peeling paintwork. I stood on a tattered raffia mat next to a small pile of abandoned plastic toys: outside things – bucket, spade, tricycle. Next to the bell was a faded sticker on the inside of the glass, a picture of a tortoiseshell kitten yawning its head off. Underneath were the words, *Beware of the Cat*.

She answered the door. We stood and stared at each other. For an unending moment, neither of us spoke. I felt my lips part, as if they wanted to whistle.

This woman was not the brittle doll of the crematorium nor the frazzled young mother in the supermarket. She was something between the two. Her look was casual but careful: black trousers and a long, linen-cotton jumper with the cuffs rolled over several times; light, immaculate make-up, mostly on the eyes; fair hair with the front section lifted up and clipped back from her face – a broad face with a wide, inscrutable mouth and knowing eyes. She had clearly gone to some trouble for me but in a way which was designed to look as if she had made no effort at all: exactly what I had done. It was like seeing my reflection in a misted or pitted glass. This woman was not me – she was something much more scary. She was what I might have been.

I'll never know whether she thought the same, but she looked as if she did.

She nodded, then stood back to allow me to step in. I opened my mouth to speak and she gestured upstairs with a pointed finger: the child. Then she led me down the hallway – woodchip wallpaper, painted light green – into a kitchen at the back of the house, where she turned and carefully pushed the door until it was almost closed but still slightly ajar. I waited while she stood by it for a moment, her head towards it in an exaggerated listening gesture.

When she eventually said something, her voice came as a slight surprise, as if a figure in a dream had suddenly spoken. 'He's fast asleep. Thank you for coming. Sit down and I'll make a drink.'

'Sorry I'm late,' I said, as I shrugged my coat off my shoulders. 'The car wouldn't start. I got the Tube but I had to walk at either end.'

'Well it worked out quite well actually, I had trouble getting him off, wasn't worn out enough. Do you have your own car or were you trying to use the Mini?'

I looked at her. 'Yes.'

She gave a small smile, an ever-so-slightly nasty smile. 'Useless, that car. The undercarriage will drop out one day.'

While she filled the kettle I took the opportunity to glance around the kitchen, which was clearly the favoured room of the house. There was evidence of a bit of money being spent; new washing-machine and cooker, nice pine table. One of the kid's scrawly drawings had been framed and hung above the counter. I had a sudden thought: *I wonder if the child is Peter's.*

At the back door, I could hear a very faint mewing and scratching, probably the cat of which I was to beware.

As the visitor, I felt I was allowed the luxury of silence. She was the one who wanted to see me, after all. The remark about the Mini had been making a point, laying out the terms of reference. I had got the message, now it was up to her. We sat at her table in silence for some moments, nursing our cups of coffee in our hands, as if we were cold. I noticed that we were subconsciously copying each other's gestures. Any minute now, she would confide in me.

'Peter and I . . .' she began. 'Peter and I were involved.'

'How long ago?' I asked.

'Before you,' she said quickly. 'Quite some time before. When he died, I hadn't seen him for nearly a year. I only found out he had died by accident, in fact. Local man in fatal car crash. It mentioned the car so I rang someone to find out.' She exhaled shortly through her nose, then gave a half-smile. 'That's the reason I came to the crematorium really, to be sure. I didn't believe it you see. Although I knew it was a pretty stupid thing to do – they'd be there of course. That's why I was so nervous. I must have seemed a bit bonkers to you. I didn't really know what to say. When I saw you with them . . .' Her voice trailed off. She looked down into her coffee cup, still cradled in her hands.

When she looked up again she was staring straight ahead and her face had taken on a blank but purposeful expression. Her voice was clear. 'I wanted to dance on his grave.'

Outside in the street, there was the low rumble of a passing lorry. When its noise had faded, I became aware of the gentle, fuzzy hum of the fridge to my left and the contrastingly tinny, mechanical tick of the wooden clock on the wall behind her. She took another sip from her drink but did not speak.

'Do you know anything about bearer shares?' I asked her.

She came round and looked at me, her gaze coming back into focus. 'What?'

'What did Peter do with Sophie and Alex?'

She made a small derisive sound in her throat. 'If I were you I would steer well clear of them, although maybe they've got their teeth into you already. They ran a business together, the three of them, well Peter and Alex really. Sophie couldn't run a car, never mind a business, she's just there for show, just to be nice to people and make it all seem homey and cosy. I suppose you got the routine about the sofa?' I looked at her. She mimicked Sophie's voice, lightly, with a slight trill. 'Oh Peter, you're always so rude about our sofa. I think it's lovely. I like soft things, but then I suppose we are a bit soft and fluffy, me and Alex.'

I was smiling but I was in pain. Up until then, this woman's association with Peter had not bothered me. I had wondered if her child was his. I had registered that she had used Peter's Mini. But at the mention of the sofa I felt a pang as sharp as if she had leaned over and prodded me with one of her long-nailed fingers. She must have known Peter so much better than I did. She even knew him well enough to dislike his friends. I was the new kid on the block by comparison. What on earth must she think of me?

'Why did you want to dance on Peter's grave?'

She wouldn't look me in the eye. 'He wasn't a very nice man. I don't like telling you all this because maybe you hadn't found out yet but you would have done sooner or later. I wouldn't have dared ring you up. But someone I spoke to at the crematorium said you had only just met him so I thought maybe it was all right. There wouldn't have been time. I don't know how close you are to the Littletons . . .' She faltered to a halt.

'I didn't know you were living in the house,' she continued. 'But I guessed when I saw you in the supermarket. You wouldn't have been buying all that food if you were just passing. I drove past a couple of times later that day and saw the Mini in the drive and the lights on. Once I saw you come out in your slippers and get something you had forgotten from the back seat. You seemed very at ease. I didn't really understand. That's why I am taking a risk. You could just go back to the Littletons and tell them everything and then I'd get one of his nasty phone calls. But then I thought, what have I got to lose?'

She had begun to look frightened.

'I'm living in the house,' I said, 'because it belongs to me.'

Her jaw nearly hit her nice pine table.

'Peter made a will leaving everything to me. I only found out after he was killed. It was as big a shock to me as it was to everybody else, believe you me. I'm still finding out about him. But you can relax. The Littletons don't have any hold over me. Quite the reverse in fact. They want some stuff from the house, I don't know what.' To my surprise, I realised that despite my gentle tone of voice I was thinking fiercely, *he loved me, not you. He left all his money to me. So there. That proves it.* There was no reason for me to tell her about the will. I may have sounded soft and confiding but my motives were malicious. I had something to prove.

Her face betrayed a brief and swiftly changing register of thought: shock, dismay, resignation – then, more gradually, pleasure. 'That means,' she said thoughtfully, 'that it was all coming apart.' She pursed her lips, then made a low chuckling sound in her throat, without moving a muscle on her face. 'My God,' she said, 'they must have died.' Her eyes were gleaming.

Then she glanced over at me as if she was only just remembering my presence. She spoke firmly. 'When Peter died,' she said, 'he had something belonging to me. I want you to let me come over to the house and get it.'

'What is it?'

'I'd rather not say.'

'Look,' I said, 'ever since he died people have been trying to get something out of me. If you want to turn that house over, you're going to have to get in the queue.'

Her voice rose. 'I don't want to turn it over I just want to get something and come straight back out again. It'll take five minutes, probably.'

'Do you know where it is?'

Her voice faltered. 'Probably . . .'

Did she hell. The sceptism on my face must have showed because, suddenly, she lost it.

'It's *nothing* you could want. *Nothing* of any value to you. You've got that whole bloody house now and good riddance but what the hell did you do for it? You hardly knew him. I've been through hell! You've no idea what I've been through.'

'Precisely,' I said coolly.

She got to her feet. Her face held the fury of one who has suffered and is incredulous that the person she is speaking to does not appreciate her suffering. 'You think you're something special,' she said venomously, leaning towards me over the table, 'because you've got off scot-free. Well I've news for you. You're not. You're just lucky. In the right place at the right time. If Peter didn't screw you over well then bully for you but it was just a matter of time, darling, believe you me!'

I rose to my feet slowly and picked up my coat. When I am angry I become very calm, and very lucid. 'I am sorry I can't help you,' I said lightly. 'But I am sure you will appreciate that when a complete stranger rings me up and wants to go through the house I am living in I feel entitled to ask a few questions. If you don't want to answer then that's fine by me.'

She burst into tears.

We both sat down again while she had a good cry. She sobbed moistly, fumbling in both her sleeves for a tissue. When she couldn't find one she began to gulp with some anxiety. I looked around the kitchen. On the surface to my right was a kitchen roll, impaled on a pine kitchen-roll stand. I rose and tore off a sheet. It had a pattern along both edges: tiny red triangles. She took it from me and blew her nose. She didn't say thank you.

From upstairs came the distant, insistent wail of a toddler who has woken up and cannot understand why his mother is not standing by the cot, waiting to administer his every need.

She blew her nose again. 'Excuse me . . .' she mumbled damply, scrunching up the piece of kitchen towel in her fist and stuffing it in her sleeve. She rose and wiped underneath her eyes with the back of her index finger. 'I won't be a minute.' She left the room.

I sat back in my chair, feeling mean, feeling like the playground bully. Distantly, from behind the back door, there came the thin, unoptimistic mewing of the cat. I rose from my seat and saw that outside it had begun to rain. I went over and grasped the door handle to open it and let the cat in. At the sound of my approach the animal cried out, desperate and pleading. I turned the handle but the door was locked. I went back to my seat.

She returned after a few minutes with the boy sitting cosily in the crook of her right arm and leaning his head against her chest, his fist crammed into his mouth. The rest of his hand and his plump little arm were shiny with saliva. His fringe was damp and skewed across his forehead and his gaze vacant. He was barely awake. His misty round eyes regarded me for a moment, then he turned and buried his head in his mother's jumper.

She had regained her composure. She glanced at me.

There is nothing like having a child in their arms to make some women look self-satisfied. You may have something I want, her glance said, but I have this, and I want this more than anything.

I rose to my feet.

She said. 'I'm sorry if I lost my temper. If you knew, you'd understand. Can I call you tomorrow when I've calmed down a bit?'

'Yes,' I said, 'of course.'

We both turned and went out into the hallway.

At the front door, we paused. 'Can I just ask you something?' I said.

She looked at me.

I held her gaze. 'Are you afraid of Sophie and Alex?'

She paused, and for a second or two we were caught in the moment, strung on each other's gaze, in the way we had been when she had first opened the door and we had looked at each other, wondering.

'Yes,' Iris said. 'I am.'

*

I feel as though I'm being followed.

Iris pauses, looking down into her coffee, where a few grains of chocolate powder and brown sugar have formed a muddy swirl in an unconvincing froth of cream. Her tone is uncertain. Somebody who did not know her very well might be unable to decide whether or not she is joking.

Susan knows her very well indeed – and knows that she is not. 'Do you mean,' she asks carefully, 'that you think you're being followed or just that you feel as though you are?'

Iris looks up and to one side. In the light from the window her face looks pale and grey, her skin translucent. There are fine veins in her cheeks, visible imprints of the cold and unpredictable weather outside. Her nose is red. All week, it has been windy. Her hands have been dry and her face both chapped and clammy, like that of a corpse.

The rims of her eyes are pinkish. When Iris is worried, she has a slightly rodent quality. 'I don't know,' she says. 'That's what makes it all so difficult. Being haunted is straightforward. That's all in the head isn't it? I'm used to that. I'm used to my head playing tricks on the rest of me. I keep looking straight ahead and wait for the storm to pass. That's what I've always done. It hasn't been very nice but I've managed. No more difficult than waiting for a migraine to pass. But recently, I don't know, there's been a bit more to it. Things have been happening.'

'What sort of things?'

Iris is on the verge of tears. She keeps her face turned towards the white square of window on the left of their table, as if the act of turning it forwards might tip the balance and break the careful equilibrium of her composure; as if she is held together by that most precarious of forces – surface tension.

Her voice almost cracks. 'Things . . . stupid things. I had a blackout in the pub. My phone keeps ringing and there's no-one there. Or I mean there is someone there but no-one answers. I can tell – it isn't a normal connection but they listen to me saying my name. When I leave the building at night I hear, not exactly footsteps but a rushing sound, as if somebody's rushing along a nearby corridor, getting closer. I broke into a run last night but then I had to stop because I couldn't hear the sound if I ran and if you can't hear it then you can't work out how close it is. I don't know which is worse.'

She makes a small noise. 'Ridiculous isn't it?'

She lifts her coffee cup in both hands and nurses it for a moment, then puts it down. 'So far it's just been at work. I think it's just been at work but it's getting difficult to tell. I think there's something in that building but I don't know whether it can leave or not, God knows what I'll do if it follows me home. I'm nervous at home but I think that's just because it's making me nervous all over the place.

'It's like getting an infection. I've started looking at people on the tube, working out who's behind me on the platform, making a mental note of what people are wearing so that I can tell later how long they've been near me – a man in a dark, unbuttoned coat, a woman holding the *Financial Times*. Stupid. They probably think I'm following them.'

She gives a minuscule, self-mocking smile. 'God knows

84

where it will all end up. I'll get arrested. The neighbours will tell the newspapers I was a quiet woman who kept herself to herself.'

The tension has dissipated. Iris is determined to laugh at herself and while she is doing that there is nothing anyone can do to help her.

Next to her, there is the sound of somebody clearing their throat. Iris looks up. A man in a baggy suede coat is standing by her shoulder. He is wearing a flat cap and a great deal of grey stubble and is staring at her, moist-eyed. With a large, knotty hand, he gestures at the seat opposite her, which is empty. 'Sit down?' he asks.

Iris glances around the café, which is virtually deserted. There is no reason for him to want to sit at her table other than to sit opposite her. Kenneth's Café is a place where she doesn't normally get bothered, where she can sit alone at her usual table and stare into the window and think. It is tucked down an alleyway. She cannot begin to imagine how they make a living.

Annoyed, she rises from her seat and bends to pick up her bag from the floor.

The old man sits down in the chair opposite her. He is disappointed that she is going but pleased that he has bothered her enough to make her move. She glares at him as she turns towards the counter to pay for her unfinished coffee. He beams gummily in reply.

Iris checks her watch as she pushes out of the door, back

into the chafing cold which greets her with a blast. Two-twenty. She has overrun her lunch hour and this afternoon is her last completely free stretch before the two-day Internet course she is giving at the Infotech Training Centre. Always the same: another rash of articles in the nationals and everybody ringing up in a panic wanting to know how to do it – a self-perpetuating business, information technology, built-in obsolescence made into a fine art.

Just as she reaches the steps of her building, it begins to rain.

In the entrance hall, Tomlinson is standing at the pigeonholes, carefully inserting a few items of late post into the appropriate slots. Iris pauses, waiting to see if he has anything for her and wondering if she should try to engage him in conversation. She hovers at his shoulder, unsure whether he has realised that she is behind him.

Eventually he says without turning, 'Young man asking for you while you were out.'

'A young man?' Iris echoes idiotically.

'Well, young sort of. Told him you were out. Said he'd try again some other time. Said he was just passing.'

'Did he leave a message of any sort?'

Tomlinson sighs, which Iris takes to mean two things: one, there was no message and two, as far as he is concerned this conversation is now at an end.

Back in her office, she tries to script her introduction for the seminar. Her opening chat takes about twenty minutes and as long as she gets that right then the rest of the day will be a breeze. First impressions are everything. Her audience will be an array of businessmen, mostly under duress. She will feel an unnerving desire to don an apron and serve them spotted dick. Sometimes, she has difficulty keeping them quiet. It is essential to be completely calm and relaxed and authoritative in the opening session, otherwise the whole day becomes unpredictable.

This week has not been too bad, not so far anyway. A deadline makes everything easier. It is possible to focus, and the point of focusing is not merely to make something visible but to blur out everything else. The only cloud this week is her trip to the GP. George has made her promise to go and she has been secretly glad to be bullied. She just wishes it wasn't this afternoon. She is going to have to leave work early.

When people first used the telephone, she types, *they had to work out how to hold it and speak into it. Now it's like breathing. By the end of today, you're going to feel the same way about the Internet.* She pauses and sighs. *There are people who don't like using the phone* she continues *but how many of them do you do business with?*

The telephone rings. Iris stops. After five rings, the answer-machine will kick in. She has less than two hours to finish her preparation. There is every reason to leave the phone alone.

She lifts it carefully, as if it might be hot, and holds it an inch or so away from her ear. 'Hello? Iris Farrow?'

In the silence that follows, Iris becomes aware of herself. She becomes aware that when she answers the phone she says more than her name. She says her name, followed by a question mark. It is an abbreviated way of saying, *this is Iris Farrow here, at this end, but who are you?* It is a shorthand that every telephone-user understands. But now, for the brief duration of this loaded, echoey pause, Iris has time to reflect that it could have another meaning; a literal one. 'Iris Farrow?' *Is that Iris Farrow there?*

There is no such thing as silence, only an absence of noise, so Iris listens to the absence. It sounds the same as the other absences, which are now occurring at the rate of two or three times per day, although there was nothing yesterday. They have the texture of bed linen; an acre of space with a slightly roughened feel.

So far, she has just hung up each time, but this time she decides to wait it out. She has got used to the texture. She feels she has reached a place where interpretation might be possible.

The absence continues. Iris sits and listens. Fine by me, she thinks, with growing confidence, it's your bill, not mine. I don't need my line clear for anything. I could sit here and work on my seminar plan all afternoon with the phone in the crook of my shoulder, listening to you trying to frighten me, listening to you fail. She leans back in her chair.

Then it happens. The absence becomes filled with a sound so clear and distinct that she is convinced it is in the room with her, next to her ear. It is both strange and familiar, both meaningless and filled with intent. It is the first confirmation she has had that there is somebody making these calls rather than just a mechanical fault of some sort on the line.

It is the sound of someone drawing in breath.

She slams down the phone and leaps to her feet, instinctively moving back from her desk as if she might need room to strike out. Her scalp has tightened around her skull. Her chest heaves as she takes in breath. She waits for the phone to ring again.

It doesn't.

Her GP is called Dr Crewe and works in a busy practice just round the corner from the Newspaper Library, not far from home. Iris is early and Dr Crewe is running late. She ie called in fifty minutes after she has arrived.

Dr Crewe has mid-brown hair, streaked with grey, and a smile that crinkles. Her demeanour is brisk, unpatronising. Iris has only been once before, in the morning, and even then the doctor looked as though she was coming to the end of a long and busy day. While Iris describes her blackout in the pub, Dr Crewe leafs through her file, which consists of one piece of paper in a single fold of manila cardboard.

Iris finishes. Dr Crewe pauses and lifts the piece of paper out, frowning. 'When did you register with us?' she asks.

'Last month. I just came in so you could fill in the form. This is my first visit.'

'Your records haven't come over yet. I might have to ask you ...' Dr Crewe puts the piece of paper back. 'Any pain?'

Iris pauses. Dr Crewe looks at her. Iris says, 'No.'

Dr Crewe continues to ask questions while she takes Iris's blood pressure and listens to her heart. She is both efficient and incurious. Iris is overwhelmed with gratitude.

'We'll do what I call an MOT,' she says, 'check your thyroid, test for anaemia and so on, although I don't think that's very likely. Slip your shoes off and step on those scales if you don't mind.' While she notes Iris's weight, the doctor asks, 'Have you just moved into the area?'

'No,' Iris says calmly. 'I had a clash of personalities with my old GP.'

Dr Crewe doesn't bat an eyelid. 'Your weight is OK,' she says, 'but it's at the bottom end of what is healthy for your height. I don't want to see it going any lower.'

Iris steps off the scales and returns to her seat. While she is bent double, lacing her boots, Dr Crewe says casually, 'Any problems sleeping?'

'Like a log,' Iris replies flatly.

It is dark by the time she leaves the surgery. She walks home slowly and carefully, not wanting to arrive too quickly, feeling strangely calm. Travelling from one space to the next is the only time she gets to relax these days. So often she is doing so many things; eating, working, researching, thinking – planning in her head. People on their own always have to plan. Being in transit is a good excuse for not planning. Keeping your wits about you on a suburban street means that you can't lose them, not until you are safely home.

As she turns the corner into her road, she sees that a

car is parked outside her house. This is not unusual. A lot of people live in her street and several of them own cars. A fair proportion also have visitors. Even so, she pauses. Then, the car's engine grinds into life. Its headlights click on, bathing the street in a halfheartedly golden light. Iris takes two steps back behind the corner. She waits.

She can hear the car turning in the road to depart in the opposite direction. When the sound of it has died away, she steps back out into the empty street and swiftly walks the fifteen yards to her front door.

She unlocks the main entrance and blunders up the stairwell, which has been unlit for as long as she has lived in the flat. She is already halfway up the stairs before the crash of the front door slamming behind her echoes through the building. Mrs Stephanotis from the ground floor will leave one of her venomous notes on the hallway table the next morning.

Iris crashes into her own flat and turns on the lights. Then she runs from room to room closing the curtains. In the sitting-room, the hooks catch on the rail and she has to yank them across. She painted the rail herself; green, badly. It has never worked properly since.

Turning, she blunders her way to the kitchen. She crosses swiftly to the unit next to her stainless steel sink. When she has reached it she stops. She pauses for a second, gulping for breath. Then she yanks open the wooden drawer in front of her. Inside there is a red plastic tray divided up into sections: a short one for teaspoons; three long ones for spoons, knives and forks; and an extra long one for implements. Iris has a wide variety of implements including a long thin Kitchen Devil knife. Even in her kitchen drawer, there are devils.

She slams the drawer shut. The force of the gesture makes a loud wooden crunch decorated with a laughing, metallic tinkle as the cutlery clatters together. It is a sound with many parts.

5

*I*ris is lying.

'Are you still going out with the helicopter pilot?' her friends wanted to know and Iris would sigh inwardly. Peter was a man trapped by his profession. He might be tall and angular, with a slightly awkward gait. He might be fussy about trimming his fingernails. He might have wide blue eyes with eyelashes as long as a cartoon cow. None of it mattered. He was The Helicopter Pilot. Peter was a man who flew up and down without the aid of wings. He fluttered and settled. He was always moving on. His job was a perfect metaphor for him; for a man; for men.

'Are you still going out with the helicopter pilot?'

'Yes,' Iris would lie, when most of the time the truth was, she didn't have a clue.

All careers are metaphors; as opposed to all jobs, which are merely ways of making a living. Iris's career involved the passing of information from one recipient to the next, like a sophisticated newspaper delivery girl, weighed down by an unappreciable load of knowledge and virtually invisible. Information is not truth, that is all ye need to know. Iris knew it in spades yet she sometimes gazed at her computer screen with all the awe of an amateur astrologer discovering the Milky Way.

Once, it had been an orderly scenario of knowledge: databases which, however huge, were always finite. Now there was the Net and the possibilities for trespass had multiplied into galaxies of choices as marvellous and kaleidoscopic as outer space. She might be a neat, emotionally atrophied woman in her orthopaedic chair in a crumbling Victorian building – but as she entered each of the Net's territories she became someone else: Iris.XXX.@compuserve.com. (The XXX's were her own, slightly unprofessional quirk, a pretence of anonymity.) Iris.XXX flew and shattered. She went out on the *World Wide Web* on a Web Crawler to check the Net Happenings archives (rather than going through the list every day, which took ages these days now that everyone was so excitable). Only the other week she had gone into the *OMRI Daily Digest* for the first time, for a client. who wanted the latest on Central Asia and Transcaucasia. Later, she had nipped into *alt.chocolate* to check the recipes from the global network of chocoholics who kept each other up to date; but here she only lurked, slightly embarrassed to be doing something so surfy. Surfers were amateurs, in her opinion; geeks. She generally stuck to the Newsnets or Telnet and always abided by Netiquette. She never asked an FAQ. Nobody had ever had to tell her to RTFM. She had never been flamed, let alone mailbombed.

She was using the Net to make a living but knew all the same that the minute she lost her sense of wonder she might as well pack up and go home. Her computer was a house with many rooms. It was like exploring a mausoleum in which every corner was inhabited – or the mansion of an absent owner stuffed to the gills with mysteries to be discovered; ghosts in the basement, crimes in the attic. It was an object, a thing, a hulk of plastic and electrical impulses – yet every bit as muddled and strange and subjective as a human heart.

'What do you do?'

'I'm an Information Systems Consultant.' That usually shut them up. But so did most people's answer to the same question.

What do you do?

I'm a solicitor.

I'm a graphic designer.

I've got my own business finding short-term accommodation for visiting Japanese businessmen.

I run a brasserie in NW1.

Earthbound. Iris liked to think of herself as different. Her sense of wonder made her feel special. But in her heart of hearts she suspected that she was just as tethered as most other people she knew. All she had were the means of travel, the passport and the road map. Her job was mainly to point other people in the right direction and give a gentle shove. Her skin was too good for a hacker and she bought her underwear in Selfridges. There was no chance of finding her amongst the anoraks at the Cyber Café. People went into the information business for two reasons: as a means to an end – or because they were nerds. Iris knew she could only aspire to nerdishness. She was a woman oppressed by her own normality. Earthbound.

Peter took off. That was what she thought when she first met him, at a Sunday afternoon house-warming party in Edgware.

'What do you do?'

'I'm a helicopter pilot.'

Iris's smile split her face from ear to ear. He said it so matter-of-factly she thought he must be making it up. 'You take off,' she stated, impressed and a little bewildered.

He smiled back. 'Well I wouldn't be much of a pilot if I never left the ground.'

They were crammed into a corner of a sitting-room. The party had suddenly filled up. The hosts were running around fetching drinks and looking relieved. Alex and Sophie were newly-weds who had spent their first year of married life lodging with Alex's mother. Now safely installed in their first home, they were celebrating with the gusto of airmen recently liberated from Colditz. Iris watched them from her corner and thought how much more enthusiastic they seemed than at the wedding, as if buying a house was an infinitely more genuine and positive cause for celebration. She didn't know them very well. They were friends of friends.

Peter had been there for as long as Iris, but she noticed him only when he was backed into her corner by the incoming rush of new arrivals. Her first glance of him had been of a wide, tall back, slightly bony-looking in an off-white linen shirt, with dark, wayward curls of hair in need of trimming at the nape of the neck.

'Who do you fly for?' she asked, in a sober voice intended to demonstrate that she was not as silly as her first remark had made her appear.

'The NHS,' he said. 'Air ambulance. We operate from the London Hospital. Not as dramatic as it sounds, actually, mostly it's sitting around.' She could tell by his overtly casual tone that he loved it, that he wouldn't dream of doing anything else.

She was holding a packet of ten cigarettes and had been in the process of withdrawing one when Peter had turned and introduced himself. She saw his eyes light upon it. She offered him the packet.

'No thanks, I've given up,' he said, as he took one.

He handled the movement rather badly. They were both holding glasses of white wine. Iris had taken him seriously and started to withdraw the packet. He reached out with one hand and missed, made another quick movement and slopped a little wine onto his shirt. The joke did not quite work but Iris smiled nonetheless and registered, *this is a man who says one thing and does another*.

'I have this theory,' he said, leaning back after she had lit their cigarettes, 'it isn't smoking that gives you cancer,' he exhaled, 'it's going into the newsagent's and buying them. As long as you don't do that, you'll be fine.'

She nodded and added, slightly quickly, 'I only smoke at parties too.'

He smiled at her and she knew that he had noticed her anxiety, her eagerness to get this one sorted out – the importance of letting him know that they felt the same way on this issue. A small rule was established. He would make a witticism or a statement. Her role would be to affirm it, to agree.

She had wanted him, very badly, right from the beginning. The sequence had been immaculate. When she had first seen him, even though it was only from behind, she had wanted him physically. When he had turned and spoken to her, her interest had broadened. When he had taken the cigarette with that uncertain, half-embarrassed clumsiness, she had fallen in love with him for doing something which – she knew already – was characteristic. Having made himself momentarily vulnerable, he had then recovered himself and given an illogical but charming justification for doing exactly as he pleased. In less than two minutes, they had mapped out the entire progress of their relationship, in the same way that an Elizabethan masque describes the plot before the actors engage on the play. For Iris, it was all sewn up.

And for Peter? She asked him once, about their first encounter. It was four months into their relationship and he was out of love with her already. She asked the question too late. He shrugged. 'I bummed a cigarette off you, didn't I?' he replied.

Like most pilots, Peter had a military background, in his case naval training from the age of eighteen. If you went into the airforce, he explained, they tried to put you in a jet. He had never wanted to fly anything except helicopters.

She visited him at work once. She went to the hospital one Sunday afternoon, the quiet time when there was a lot of sitting around and Peter said the lads would be only too pleased to see a pretty face. As she came out of Whitechapel Tube Station she saw the helipad immediately, on top of the hospital, suspended like a huge trampoline. Just looking at it made her stomach lurch. She was afraid of heights.

In a busy Casualty area it took her several minutes to get the receptionist's attention. The man standing next to Iris was drunk. He had blood running down his face. He was snarling at the people behind the desk, 'Just fix it, will yer. Just fix it.' The receptionist stood and called out in a bored tone of voice, 'Can someone move him please.' Then she flapped a hand at Iris and said, 'Lift there on the right. Fifth floor. Then two flights of stairs.' Iris hurried down the corridor.

She came out of a large door, onto the roof, just as Peter and another pilot were emerging from a small door in a long brick hut built to one side. They were both dressed in orange flying suits which gave them astronautical bulk and the air of authority that uniforms always have for those who have never worn them. His face lit up (it was still early days) and he grabbed her, planting a brief, full kiss on her mouth.

'We're on a call,' he said, pushing her away and turning to a silver metal staircase that leads up to the helipad. 'Come and watch us take off.'

She followed them gingerly up the fragile, noisy staircase, glancing backwards only briefly at the dizzying spread of city several hundred feet below.

The shiny-yellow, snub-nosed helicopter sat in the middle of a yellow circle painted on the square grey pad. To Iris it looked disturbingly like the model one that her brothers had owned when they were children – just bigger. Dimly she thought, I expected it to have more bits on.

As Peter and the other pilot swung themselves into the front seats a doctor and a paramedic ran from the other side of the pad and clambered into the back. Two firemen wearing helmets and carrying green extinguishers came to see them off. One of them noticed Iris and waved her back. She retreated to the far side of the pad and stood clutching her jacket around her. At ground level it had been a mild day but up here the wind blew fiercely. It was cold.

The rotor blades began to turn, quickening rapidly to a deafening blur. Through the glass front of the helicopter she could see Peter lifting a hand to check an instrument above his head, nodding. The air around the machine flattened, span and spread – a nearby wind sock twisted wildly and an extractor pipe which was billowing a panic-stricken cloud of steam began to shudder. Iris's hair was blown back from her face. Her eyes watered.

Then, the helicopter lifted slightly. Iris's heart twisted with apprehension. The helicopter hung for a moment, suspended two or three feet above the pad, then rose swiftly, tipped at an alarming angle and veered away.

For a second it seemed enormous: a huge, yellow insect plastered against the sky. Then rapidly it shrank, becoming smaller and smaller, so tiny it turned black. Then it was a speck, then nothing. As it disappeared, the bedlam of the rotor blades faded into a fizzing noise underlain by a high-pitched, dying whine.

Then there was silence.

Iris was alone on the helipad. The firemen had gone back to their hut. She walked out into the centre, to the middle of the yellow circle, then turned slowly. All around, there was a vast view of London: Canary Wharf, the Post Office Tower, a football field with a few black figures jumping and running, Victorian ruins, churches, cranes. She stood in the centre of the circle with her arms wrapped round herself, feeling soft and pink and human, and very small. She looked up at the silent, empty sky.

There were many things that Iris remembered about her relationship with Peter. But what she remembered most was not a visual image or a smell or a word spoken out of turn. It was a general feeling, a wash which coloured the whole of her time with him and all the moments since. What she remembered was the humiliation.

Their time together had lasted less than a year and comprised two months of mutual, passionate bliss, one month of uncertainty and six of misery. They both knew that it had been a terrible mistake – but Peter realised it first.

In retrospect, what hurt her more than anything was the ordinariness of her story (along with the unworthiness of its object). She could not understand how she had let her life be destroyed by such a mundane tragedy. She knew women who had been deserted for seventeen-year-olds and left to raise two children, women who had been beaten: her cousin Linda had been hospitalised by the man she lived with. (He had broken her left cheekbone with an iron. Luckily it was cold at the time.)

Peter had merely loved her, then stopped loving her.

He had lied to her a bit as well. He had been demeaning and undermining and never taken an interest in her work, other than to mention one evening that the lads wanted to know if she could tell them how to get hold of the porn on the Internet. So combined with her sense of loss was a sense of self-censure. Peter had done nothing to her that she had not allowed him to do. To her, that seemed as bad as doing it all on her own. She had no-one to blame but herself, she reasoned. So blame herself she did.

In the immediate aftermath she thought many things. She thought that she was ugly. She thought that every time she heard a helicopter buzzing overhead it was Peter and she was about to witness him crashing – slap bang – into a tall building. She thought that for a woman to remain realistic about a man's intentions she must be entirely egoless.

When they first met, Peter had been a jealous lover. He had clutched her to him. He had told her he would kill anyone else who laid a finger on her. And he had been surprised when after all that, she believed him. He was a demanding man and she, being only human, interpreted his demandingness as love – the emotional dyslexia which all women were taught from the moment they tottered from their prams. Women had self-deceit hammered into them with the same rigour and proscriptiveness with which all children were drilled in the alphabet. Women were taught that a man who made a great show of needing them was making a great show of them; when actually, he was making a great show of need.

A man's need was his strength; a woman's her weakness. When a man loved with a great passion he got the girl, won the laurels, had his sentence suspended on the grounds of provocation. A woman who loved with the same passion was a figure of fun. A woman would be forgiven her prettiness, her wit, even her manual dexterity (as long as she didn't fix the lawnmower). She would never be forgiven her credulity.

The brick hut was called the Ops Room. It contained several desks, each with its own computer terminal. Adjacent to one of the terminals was a radio box and a scattering of different coloured telephones: red, cream, grey. A small black and white television showing the empty helipad was suspended on brackets halfway up the wall. Next to it was a huge framed map of Greater London.

Three men were leaning back in chairs in front of their desks. They all stood up as Iris entered. One came forward and shook her hand, introducing himself. 'I'm Ian, you must be Peter's friend.' He nodded towards the others. 'David, Mike . . .' Then he indicated a chair next to his desk. 'Have a seat, they'll be back in a minute, they've only gone to Chiswick. Mike here will put the kettle on.'

While they waited for the crew to return they asked Iris what a nice girl like her was doing with Peter. They gave her a spare helmet to play with. They worried about whether or not she might be cold.

They dropped hints that Peter spent most of his working hours flirting with the nurses. Mike and then David began to elaborate. Ian intervened.

'We don't want Iris taking us too seriously . . .' he said, glaring at Mike.

'She knows what he's like,' Mike said. He was a young co-pilot who sat with his feet on his desk, crunching a biscuit. He looked down and muttered, 'Slimy as weasel shit.'

The two older men both swivelled their heads towards him. 'Mixed company!' said Ian sharply.

Mike pulled a face and said, 'No offence.'

Iris sat cradling her tea nervously, thinking, I am like an alien to them. They probably wonder what I eat.

At the end of Peter's shift, she sat in the front of the helicopter while he flew it back to the airbase. The take-off terrified her beyond words. She gripped the sides of her seat and shut her eyes, feeling her breath rasping against the small microphone attached to her helmet. Peter shouted to her, into his own mike, explaining things, and his voice boomed in her ears. The thin machine around her veered and shuddered.

The flight took ten minutes and throughout she was rigid with fear. After they had split up, she wondered whether that was the moment when he had begun to despise her.

Iris is in her office when the phone rings. It is about 5.00pm. She has had the answer-machine on for the past two days and it seems to be working. No calls; not just no funny messages – no calls at all. As if her caller knew whether the machine was on or not.

It has been an admin week – follow-ups on the Internet course, typing in the businessmen's responses to the questionnaires she invited them to fill in: *How would you rate the Course Leader's guidance and tuition?* They were invited to circle numbers from 1 to 5, ranging from poor to excellent. Most of them had circled excellent out of sheer gallantry. Iris knew she had been nothing of the sort.

There was a dullness behind her eyes. She had looked in the mirror on the morning of the first day of the seminar. Her eyes were dull. The light had gone out, as if she was trying to hide inside the dark cavity of her own thoughts. Blackout.

At the end of this week there is another course, which she will also lead with her excellent powers of guidance and tuition. The thought makes her want to put her forehead on her desk and weep.

The voice leaving a message becomes recognisable in waves. Firstly, it is female. Secondly, it is young and slightly husky. Thirdly and most importantly, it is Susan.

'Listen Slagface, why haven't you rung me for months on end? Well it feels like months . . .' Susan. Iris feels overwhelmed with emotional need. If I can explain, she thinks, then Susan will be able to explain back. She has done that so often before: taken something blurry and handed it to Susan so that Susan could refract it, make it comprehensible to the ordinary gaze. Susan was able to take any sort of emotional mess and divide it up, like the piece of Stilton which Iris had once observed her eat in a pub in Fulham, cutting out the rotten bits and pushing them to one side, so that she could enjoy the flavour without the unpleasantness.

If I tell her what is wrong, Iris thinks, Susan will know what to do.

'Hi Susan.' Iris has a laugh in her voice.

Susan whoops. 'Bloody hell you're actually there. Well well. You're not dead after all.'

'No, I'm not dead. Hi.'

There is a momentary pause for both of them to register an unspeaking delight at the nearness of each other; the mutual reciprocity of that pleasure – and pleasure that it is mutual.

'How are you?' Susan asks.

'Fine . . .' Iris replies. This is the moment, the moment when she teeters on the edge of an explanation. Even as she draws breath to speak, Iris can feel herself staggering in the air, metaphorically windmilling her arms in reverse circles so that she won't fall forwards. In actual fact, she only realises what she is doing seconds later, but the end effect is the same. Iris finishes her sentence in the worst possible way. 'Fine, just working too hard that's all. How are you?'

In this day and age, Iris thinks as Susan answers, nobody should be fobbed off by somebody telling them that they are working too hard. Everybody is busy, after all, but only the professional middle classes use it as an excuse not to be human. Shop assistants are busy. Mineworkers generally have their hands full. People who clean the streets don't have an awful lot of time to spare. But Iris is well-spoken and self-employed, so for her being busy is the grand, catch-all, get-out clause of all time. Working too hard. Why? What is she working too hard to avoid?

Susan is a wonderful woman but she is not a trained therapist and anyway Iris has asked her a question. So she answers.

Susan is not fine. Susan is a bit cheesed off. Her boss is getting her down and she has just been told that her house needs underpinning in the non-too-distant future. 'I feel as though someone has told me my backside needs upholstering,' she moans. 'I'm only twenty-eight for God's sake, I can't be doing with all this.'

Susan gets her problems off her chest. Then she feels better. That's the way she likes to work. Then she says, 'Actually, I didn't ring to tell you about my upholstery. I rang to tell you that we're all very worried about you.'

Iris can feel her uncertainties inside her torso, as if her chest cavity has just caved in. Never judge somebody until you have actually hung up the phone – I must remember that, she thinks.

'Who is "we"?' she sighs.

'You know damn well and don't take that tone of voice with me. You haven't rung for months. Philip hasn't heard from you either. I bumped into him in the queue at Homebase last weekend.'

'Buying more carpet?' Philip is the older of Iris's two younger brothers. The other one is called Paul. They both married very young and produced instant menageries of children. Philip has a mania for replacing carpets. His house is like the Severn Bridge. No sooner is one end done than Philip starts on the other. He knows more about tuftpile than any man alive.

'Iris. Why are you always so nasty about Philip?' Susan isn't joking.

Iris chooses to ignore her. 'So what was the upshot of this little chat in Homebase? You all think I'm about to throw myself out of my office window.'

She can sense Susan's growing irritation. 'Are you going to go to Sammy's birthday party? Philip said he left a message on your machine weeks ago but you didn't reply. I thought if you were you could come round to me afterwards. It's a Sunday.'

'Why don't you come to Philip's?'

'Can't. Got to go and see my dad.' Susan's father is in the latter stages of Alzheimer's disease, in a nursing home in

Monken Hadley. Susan always refers to it matter-of-factly, without the remotest hint of self-pity.

'Oh all right then. Give me the date.' Iris reaches for her Filofax which lies open by the telephone.

'Ring Philip. Tell him you're coming.'

'Yes yes, just tell me when it is. I'll check whether I'm free.' Iris bites at the inside of her mouth and is suddenly glad that Susan cannot see the look on her face. Of course she is free. She is always free at the weekends, nowadays.

After they have made their date, Susan says. 'Someone else was asking after you the other day. I ought to get a fee.'

'Who?' asks Iris, although she is fairly certain she is not going to like the answer.

'Alex and Sophie.'

'I hope you told them to take a running jump.'

'They were in the pub,' Susan pauses, 'on their own.'

'And they thought they would enquire about poor pathetic little Iris.'

'Oh *Iris*!'

Iris mimics Susan's voice with a severity that makes it clear she is not trying to be funny. 'Oh *Iris*, why are you always so *nasty*?' By the time they hang up, Susan will be sorry she has called. With any luck.

After she has put the phone down, Iris sits at her desk with her face in her hands, for a very long time. She thinks about crying but it seems too much like hard work. She thinks about that joke she made about throwing herself out of the window of her office. Three floors up. Death would be uncertain.

On the wall above her computer is a Sasco Year Planner. It has been stuck up with Blu-Tack, ineffectually, and curves stiffly against the wall as if it is trying to crawl off on an exploration, caterpillar-fashion. At the start of each year, Iris buys a new tubular package and tips out the coloured stickers and the wash-off pen; a whole new year to unroll. Spread out on her desk, with reference manuals weighting each corner, a year planner is a grand blank of possibilities. She likes to look at obscure dates: June 23rd, September 14th, November 30th (St Andrew's Day, whoever he may be). Each rectangle is a day on which anything might happen.

Then, standing back from her desk, she is able to look down and see it all. A year. A whole year of her life laid out, as if it was nothing more than a sheet of paper. How many more of those sheets does she have left? Twelve? Twenty-two? Fifty-four? Even if it was sixty, she could still stack them in a pile then lift them here and there; flick through; glimpse. November 18th, 2003? Not much happening then. How about August 7th, 2017? Perhaps she should pencil in a dental appointment, in case she won't have died by then.

She stares up at the year on the wall in front of her and allows her gaze to run along each horizontal month. January and February are already done. It is March. For the rest of this month, the calendar is fairly full, appointments and commitments in her neat, diagonal scrawl. April is fairly busy too. In May it starts to thin out. June and July hold the odd dot of planning – the Bank Holiday she has booked for a trip to the Malvern Hills with Susan and a couple of her friends. Beyond that, the summer stretches into white space.

Her eyes follow the numbers, their inexorable undulation: up to thirty or thirty-one then back down again with a sickening plummet, like a bungee jump performed backwards. August; September; a nephew's birthday marked in optimistic isolation the first week of October; November and a date with the mysterious St Andrew; December 31st, the end.

If only we knew. If only we knew what would happen in those small, enclosed rectangles and how many sheets of paper we have left. A whole arena of planning would be open to us. It would be so much easier to prioritise. Iris is someone who likes to prioritise and it annoys hell out of her that in this respect she cannot. If Iris ever commits suicide it will not be because of despair. It will be because she organises everything and it seems ludicrous that something as important as her own death is unplannable.

I think about death all the time. I think about how it could happen at any moment – quickly, violently, unexpectedly. I think about how I should at least put my papers in order, leave a note saying I would like to be cremated. Then I think that to do that would be to invite death, like signing my own warrant. I don't want to come to terms with it. I want to pretend it will never happen.

There is nothing like a Sasco Year Planner for bringing home a sense of one's own mortality.

Iris leans back in her chair, arching her back, then slumps forward and looks at her watch. She sits up in surprise. It is nearly seven. She must have been on the phone to Susan for much longer than she realised. She frowns. Unless she has been daydreaming. Time is slipping. She shakes her head from side to side, a little. There is a slight ringing in her ears.

She rises from her seat and picks up her make-up bag from where it sits on top of her in-tray. She keeps toothbrush, paste, lipstick and other touch-up items at the office, in case she is going out straight after work. More commonly, she takes them to the ladies' toilet then finds she can't be bothered. The man sitting opposite her on the Tube is not going to care whether her teeth are clean or not.

Outside in the corridor, she pauses and glances either way with a slight sense of unease. Everything has been fine this week. She is beginning to think that there is nothing to worry about – but realising that an hour or two has slipped by without her noticing has unsettled her, as if she has skimmed over an unexpected fold in her year planner and somehow some small space of time has been lost, like a penny which has slipped down the back of a sofa.

In the ladies', she dumps her make-up bag on the shelf beneath the horizontal strip of mirror and locks herself in a cubicle. Afterwards she passes her hands back and forth underneath a rush of cold water from the hot tap. She tucks her bag under her right upper arm and pushes herself backwards through the first of two swing doors that lead out to the corridor, shaking the water from her hands.

As she emerges, she hears a bang, like a door slamming. She stops and listens. The echo of the bang is still drifting down the corridor and she wonders if it could be an echo of a noise from the inner door of the toilet – but it didn't sound as if it was coming from that direction. It sounded as though it was coming from the direction of her office.

Opposite the ladies', there is a window, a sash window with peeling paintwork. The panes of glass are so dirty you can scarcely see the view even in daylight – and the daylight has almost gone. She can only just make out the roofs below and the shapes of neighbouring buildings, a series of flat and perpendicular perspectives in uninspiring browns, like empty boxes. Looking out of that window and at the dim sky beyond, it is possible to believe that some virus has struck the city and it is now deserted, that you are the only living thing left on the planet.

Something catches the edge of her vision and she turns. The double doors that lead back to her office have round glass portholes criss-crossed with wire. For a second, tangentially, she thinks she sees a black shape, a shadow – but her gaze flickers a moment too late. In the instant it takes her to look, the image has gone. There is nothing there – but a visual imprint remains, like a feeling on the skin from a grasp which will later leave a bruise. Iris draws breath and remains very, very calm. She must walk towards

the swing doors, push them aside and return to her office.
She will not go mad.

She stands in front of the doors, her hands lifted to push
them open. They are painted with that very old, heavy
gloss paint that leaves an almost yellowish sheen. The
colour beneath is green; not light green or dark green
but dull green, the green of large institutions, hospital-sick
green. Iris steps through the doors and moves swiftly the
few steps to her office.

The door is as she left it, closed but on the latch. Without
looking down the dark, long corridor, she steps into the
white square of her office, doing three things at once;
listening for any unusual noise, glancing at the places in
her office where it might be possible to hide (under the
desk, in the corner next to the filing cabinet) and lifting
a hand to fumble at the lock.

Her office is silent and empty. On the desk, her *pending*
tray sits waiting, containing all the ordinary detail of her
business, the tiny bricks with which her life is constructed.
She leans back against the door and feels annoyed with
herself. If you do not stop this, she thinks, you are
finished.

Then she hears it – a soft tapping noise. Her head
is leaning back against the door so she feels it as well
as hears. Somebody is tapping on her door, gently but
definitely, inches away from her head.

She springs away from the door as if it might enfold her
and crosses the office to her desk. As she reaches for the
phone, she is aware that the tapping has stopped but its

cessation feels like a temporary pause, as if the hand that is tapping is suspended an inch or two away, and waiting.

Her hands are quite steady but the rest of her is shaking as she picks up the phone and dials 103, Tomlinson's room, cursing the fact that the only other human in the building is this slow little man with his unbuttoned jacket and crumbs on his lower lip.

'Hello?' Tomlinson's voice is unbearably casual.

'Hello? Hello this is Iris in 314. Look, there's someone creeping around up here.'

Tomlinson pauses to absorb this information. Iris is still frightened but his palpable lack of panic is proving helpful. Tomlinson is a man who never has nightmares, that much is obvious – and if he doesn't have his own then it is unlikely that he would consider having hers. Her breathing begins to steady.

'Look,' she says. 'Could it be a cleaner, or a maintenance man? Somebody just knocked on the door to my office. But it wasn't a normal knock. There is somebody up here.'

'Maybe I should come up and take a look round,' Tomlinson says, grudgingly. In the background, she can hear the portable television which he keeps on his desk, next to his kettle and his radio. Once, when she went down to pick up her post, he had all three going simultaneously. 'Third floor, room fourteen, are you?'

'Yes,' she says irritably. He must know that by now. 'I'm the only one on this floor aren't I? Well I'm the only one on this corridor anyway, you must know.'

'I'll be up directly, m'dear. Don't you worry now.' The

alarm in her voice has caused Tomlinson to change persona. He has gone into caring caretaker mode. 'I'll bring the keys and we'll have a little look round. Don't you worry.'

'Thank you . . . thanks.' Iris puts down the phone, already beginning to feel silly. How can a building which contains Tomlinson's mundane, crumpled little form also house her fears? The two are mutually exclusive. Shadows only exist if you notice them.

When she turns round, she does not feel silly any more. She feels cold, struck through with a chill as deep and as shattering as if she has been blasted by a bolt of lightning made out of an icicle.

Her office door is standing wide open.

6

When Tomlinson arrives, Iris is rigid in her chair. She
has not moved for over ten minutes. She is staring
straight ahead. One hand is balled into a fist and jammed
against her mouth, the other arm is wrapped around her
torso with the hand clutching the opposite shoulder. Her
face has an unearthly expression. She looks like a corpse
in a B-movie, the one that people don't realise is dead until
they touch it, when it keels over with a thump.

Iris is not dead but neither is she happy. She doesn't move
when Tomlinson appears in her doorway but after a second
her eyes turn and her gaze hits him like the beam from a
concentration camp searchlight.

'I rang a quarter of an hour ago,' she says, without
moving her fist from its position in front of her mouth.

Tomlinson steps into the office and closes the door
behind him. He frowns and moves his mouth in an
expression which suggests that he is thinking before
he speaks. 'Had a look round on my way up,' he says
eventually. 'Nothing about. Checked the other offices round
here. Turned the lights on down the corridor. The front door

117

is locked now, nothing came in during the last hour. Pretty sure everybody else is off home.'

Iris removes the fist from her mouth and her shoulders sink a little, as if somebody has let a bit of air out. She exhales. 'I didn't imagine it,' she says wearily. 'Somebody knocked at my door. Tapped. It's not the first time this kind of thing has happened. I'm sorry but something is going on. I don't know what.' She wonders if she should try to make Tomlinson concerned about her tenancy. 'I can't work in a building when I don't feel secure.' She looks at him. Then it occurs to her that his expression is slightly sheepish.

She sits up. 'Do you know anything about this?'

He frowns.

She stares at him but he won't look directly at her. His gaze wanders around the room, as if he is trying to check the walls discreetly.

'Mr Tomlinson . . .' Iris says in a measured voice. It is the first time she has addressed him directly by name. She has never known what to call him. Tomlinson on its own has always felt too imperious; Mr Tomlinson too wet.

She injects it with as much formality as she can muster given that he has just witnessed her in a state of catatonic hysteria. 'Mr Tomlinson, you look after this building and I presume you know about everything that happens. If there have been problems with intruders then I think that it's only fair you tell me about it. I would like to know whether I'm mad or not, after all.'

Tomlinson glances at his watch. 'You busy? he asks. 'Off home, or have you got a bit of time?'

Iris rises from her chair. 'No. I've got some time.'

Tomlinson nods back out into the corridor. 'We can go downstairs if you like. Put the kettle on.'

Iris nods and turns to pack up her desk. The last thing she wants to do is sit and chat up here. 'I'll come down with you,' she says over her shoulder, in case he was thinking of suggesting that she follows him down in a minute or two.

He replies in a tone of voice she has not heard him use before, a lower tone, almost kindly. 'I'm not going anywhere. I'll be right here.'

She feels the sudden, bathetic warmth of tears behind her eyes. She is glad she has her back to him and an excuse to keep it that way for a minute or so. The fear and tension have ebbed away and in their place there is an uneasy sense of relief, a vulnerability. She brushes at her face with the back of one hand, annoyed with herself. *Child*, she thinks crossly. You run your own business for heaven's sake, you own a car and flat. You have a life, you child.

Tomlinson's room is exactly how Iris has imagined it from the brief glimpses she has seen in passing. There is a floor of speckled linoleum, painted plaster walls and a huge old desk that looks as if it has come from an office circa 1955. The whole room has a fifties feel, in fact. Next to the desk is a yellow fridge with a curved chrome handle and, on top of the fridge, a portable television. A wildlife programme is in progress but the sound is turned down. A silent leopard pursues silent antelope through tall grass which waves, silently. After a few yards, the leopard gives up. There is a

119

close-up of an antelope staring out of the screen, motionless, its eyes wide and questioning.

Tomlinson goes over to the television and turns it off. He wanders behind the fridge and disappears from view. Iris can hear him turning a tap and filling a kettle. 'Sit down,' he says. His tone of voice has returned to normal.

Iris glances around then sits on a tall wooden stool which is just inside the door. Tomlinson's coat is hanging on a wire coat-hanger on the back of the door and she sees that it is a Burberry mac. It must come down to his ankles, she thinks.

Tomlinson emerges and plugs the kettle into the same multi-plug that also holds the leads for the fridge and the television. He clicks the kettle on, then busies himself with finding cups and saucers. Iris wonders whether he is just following his usual routine or whether he is pottering about because he doesn't know how to get the conversation going.

'Have you been here long?' she asks, much as she might ask somebody whose home she is visiting for the first time.

'Seventeen years,' Tomlinson replies. 'They put me at the back to start off with but it weren't any good.'

She has the feeling that line of conversation is something of a dead end.

At the back of the room there is another door; a toilet, Iris supposes. She thinks about her image of him sleeping in the basement on a pallet bed. 'I think of you almost as a part of the building,' she says, her voice raised slightly

in a lighthearted tone which is intended to suggest that
she is only being jovial. 'You always seem to be here. I
half imagined you slept in the basement.'

Tomlinson glances at her in the act of pouring water
into the cups, with a slightly-annoyed, slightly-puzzled
expression on his face, as if he thinks she is a bit mad.
'I live in Bexleyheath,' he says.

Iris decides not to make any more attempts at chit-chat.

He brings her tea over and hands it to her, then opens
the top drawer of the metal filing cabinet on her left. He
lifts out a maroon-coloured biscuit tin with a picture of a
coach and horses on the front. He prises the lid open and
withdraws a packet of chocolate biscuits. Iris has the same
brand at home: German, square-shaped, with a layer of
very dark, bitter chocolate which is thicker than the biscuit
underneath.

As he offers her one, she wonders if that can really be a
flick of amusement she sees on his face.

'I suppose you thought I'd eat Digestives, didn't you?'
he says.

She takes one and looks at him. 'Yes,' she says frankly,
'I did.'

He gives an uneven grin and Iris realises that the question
was a sort of test. If she had tried to be tactful and lied about
her own snobbery, she would have failed. Polite conversation was not the way to earn Mr Tomlinson's respect.
Straightforward honesty was much more effective.

Iris eats her square German biscuit and drinks her tea
while Tomlinson goes over to a cupboard on the wall, opens

it and takes out a pile of papers. He begins to rummage through. Iris shivers lightly, even though she is wearing her coat. There is a small window opposite her and it is open. Outside, it is dark.

'Thought it was here . . .' Tomlinson says. He has pulled out a stiff, shiny booklet with a black cover and white lettering. He brings it over to her. There is a black and white photograph of a church on the front and the title reads, *Historic Buildings of the City of London*. It is the sort of booklet they sell in the shops of museums and art galleries. She puts her tea down on top of the filing cabinet and takes it from him.

'Page thirty-seven,' he says. 'I think it's thirty-seven.'

She flicks through the booklet. It is mostly photographs, with accompanying text in a large typeface. On page thirty-seven there is the picture of a large Victorian building with pillars either side of the door and three stone steps leading up to the entrance. The caption underneath reads, *Asylum of the Holy Redeemer, WC1*.

Iris looks up from the booklet at Tomlinson, her eyes wide. 'Here?' she asks. 'There used to be a lunatic asylum here?'

'Bit more to it than that,' Tomlinson says. 'The facade has been rebuilt, as you can see from that, and you can't tell but the wings were added. But the foundations were the same, that's why the steps are still there. The basement of this building has been unchanged since it was built. There's a level below where we keep all the old desks and stuff. The cells are still there, the cells where they used to keep people.

Tiny they are. You wouldn't keep a dog there nowadays. There's still the marks for the posts where they used to chain people to the wall.'

Iris reads the text opposite the picture. *In its prime, in the 1890's, the asylum held nearly eight hundred men, women and children, including the criminally insane. Malnutrition and disease were rife amongst the inmates, as was, according to the Sedgewick Report of 1902, promiscuity. 'It is well known,' he wrote in his conclusion, 'that the mad have no sense of shame.'*

She looks at Tomlinson, scrutinising his face, noticing how thick his eyebrows are, how small and dark the pupils of his eyes. She searches for some sort of physical sign that he is trustworthy but he seems as inscrutable as ever, returning her gaze calmly. 'What are you saying?' she demands.

He takes the book from her and puts it down on the desk. 'You can take that home with you if you want,' he says as he turns away. He walks towards the door on the other side of the room. Halfway there he turns back and beckons her. She rises from the stool and follows.

The door opens onto a large cupboard. The cupboard is lined with shelves and the shelves are full of books. Tomlinson flicks a light switch and a bare bulb illuminates their spines. The ones on the top shelves look brown and ancient. Some of them have library lettering on the bottom of the spines. Lower down they become more modern, mostly paperbacks. On the bottom shelf, which is at knee height, there are stacks of old, sepia-coloured newspapers.

'You might call it a hobby of mine,' Tomlinson says. 'The wife won't let me keep them at home. Gives her the creeps she says. Bit of a pain really when you want to discuss things with people. I can hardly get people to come here. I don't think I should have them here really, some of them are probably worth a bit.'

As Iris steps into the cupboard, he reaches out and withdraws a book from one of the upper shelves, a small green pamphlet with a tattered cover. He hands it to her. It is a volume of PROCEEDINGS OF THE SOCIETY FOR PSYCHICAL RESEARCH and is called *Six Theories About Apparitions*. She opens it carefully, glancing at Tomlinson to make sure it is all right. He doesn't attempt to stop her so she leafs slowly through the clotted-cream-coloured pages. On one of them, there is a blue, circular British Library stamp. On another, there are some pencilled notes in the margin, written in a neat but tiny and illegible hand. About halfway through, there is a table called 'Types of Apparitions and Their Distinctive Traits: Percentage Distributions'. Reading it, she sees that apparitions of persons dead less than twelve hours have a fifty-nine-per-cent chance of giving evidence of the death of the appearer.

'I like Hart,' Tomlinson says. 'He was old school. All based on Gurney of course. Some of this stuff . . .' he waves a hand at the paperbacks, 'rubbish some of it, sensationalist. Books called things like "How to Become Psychic".' He snorts through his mouth like a horse. 'Lot of nutters into this kind of thing.'

Iris hands the pamphlet back to him and looks up at

the shelves. 'This is an amazing collection,' she says, her professional interest in the assembly of knowledge momentarily overcoming the more immediate concern. She picks out a paperback from the lower shelves. It is called *Phone Calls From Beyond the Grave*. On the front there is a shiny illustration of a skeleton holding a telephone receiver to the side of its skull. Its eyes glow red. The lettering of the title drips blood.

'Can't say I'm convinced by apparitions that use new technology,' Tomlinson sniffs. 'How are they supposed to have learnt how to do it? You wouldn't credit some of it. EVP. Thoughtography. Wide open to abuse in my opinion, although some put it in the poltergeist category. Some bloke, you know, claimed he'd picked up thousands of messages on his shortwave radio but he knew about sixteen different languages so if you listened long enough I would say you could make sense out of just about anything.'

Iris puts *Phone Calls From Beyond the Grave* back in its place. She is still scanning the shelves as she speaks. 'Are you saying you think this building is haunted?' she asks.

'I know it is,' Tomlinson replies. 'I've seen it myself.

As a child, Iris had believed in ghosts. She had treasured her convictions in secret, knowing that they would be mocked by her parents, nurturing them in the same way that she cared for her plastic doll which cried and drank and wet itself. She had enjoyed the belief that she had fallen upon a secret truth, something of her own creation, hers and hers alone. She was disappointed when she realised that all other children believed in ghosts as well.

Then later, in her adult years, she thought, I only believed in them as a child because I had no history. I was seduced by the idea of an entity which was all history and no future.

Not that she had had any sense of the future herself. For Iris, childhood had been composed solely of the wide, interminable present. The earth was as flat as a pancake.

She is twenty-seven years old, now, and the earth is round: this much her mind will encompass. It will also encompass the idea that all knowledge is accessible from a plastic box which sits on her desk, conjurable in pin pricks of light by the pressing of a series of buttons. There are limits, however, and her thought processes have just bumped up against one of them.

'I don't believe in ghosts,' she says.

'Neither do I,' Tomlinson retorts.

She looks at him.

'Not in the way you mean anyway,' Tomlinson has the remnants of a sigh in his voice, as if this is something he has had to explain quite a few times before. 'Most people think that if you say you believe in ghosts then you believe in some bloke with a beard or some woman in a floaty dress who points a pointy finger and tells you to beware or says they were murdered by the squire or some such. I think its codswallop. But I'll tell you what I saw. And I can tell you what I think it is.'

'Where did you see it?'

'I can show you if you like.' He gestures back into the other room. Iris goes out and Tomlinson turns the cupboard light off and shuts the door behind him. Then he beckons her over to where his tea sits, half-drunk, on the desk. He points at it. She looks into the teacup, wondering helplessly if he is seriously trying to tell her that he has seen a ghost in it.

While she is gazing at the tea, he goes over to the biscuit tin and takes out a biscuit. Then he comes back to the desk and pushes around the pile of old papers in which he found the booklet. He places a piece of blank paper next to the tea-cup, then dips the biscuit in the tea and shakes it over the piece of paper. A few spurts of tea drop onto it and smear. He points.

'See those marks,' he says, 'the brown stains on the paper? What do they tell you about the tea, or the biscuit, or the cup? What do they tell you about why we drink tea, about us?'

She shakes her head.

'That's what ghosts are,' Tomlinson says. 'They're like those marks on the paper. They're flickerings, nothing, scraps of information, either things you see or hear but so briefly they don't mean anything. They're like tapes that snag and replay on tape machines then get stuck in a loop and can't go any further. That's why they walk through walls or don't seem to see you. Anyone who says a ghost spoke to them needs their head seeing to. They're just flashes that got stuck in time somehow. There's no more reason to be scared of them than you would if you found that piece of paper in fifty years' time and wondered what those marks on it were.'

He turns and heads for the door, out to the entrance hall. She wonders if he is going to get something, then realises as he steps out that she is expected to follow. She goes after him. 'Where are we going?' she asks as she catches up. He has paused to click on a set of eight metal light switches in the entrance.

'To show you where I saw it,' he replies, 'that's what you wanted wasn't it?'

'What? Where?'

'Basement of course.'

They stride down the ground-floor corridor, past the rows of closed and locked office doors, to the back stairs. Tomlinson walks quickly and confidently. Iris walks quickly, keen to stay physically close, as if it might be possible to reach out for his powers of rationality if anything untoward should happen. She feels strangely unfrightened. She feels a sense of triumph. She has the power of movement and understanding and this thing – whatever it is – according to Tomlinson, has no power.

At the bottom of the back stairs there is another metal rectangle of light switches. Tomlinson pauses and flicks the first row. It is the wrong row and for a second the lights on the stairs go off and they are plunged into darkness. Then he flicks the whole set on and a fluorescent strip above them pings into life – bright, white, twentieth-century life. Double doors lead through into the basement.

The basement ceiling is lined with more fluorescent strips and the first room is very long and filled with row after row of metal stack shelving, mostly jammed with maroon-coloured box files which are coated with an opaque fur of thick grey dust. 'God knows what all this stuff is,' Tomlinson says as they make their way down the stacks. 'Could be anything here. It was an insurance firm I think. Then some time it got bought up by these property people who own it now, probably thought they were going to do it up and make a bomb. Then you had all that recession business. Can't give away office space these days, not even new stuff. Nobody wants this sort of building except people who can't afford anything proper.' He catches himself. 'Present company excepted of course.'

'I can't afford anything proper,' Iris says drily.

They are approaching another set of doors. Iris pauses. A small exercise book is hanging from the knob by a piece of string. Attached to it, by another piece of string, is the stub of a pencil. She lifts the book up. On the front of it, written in capitals, is SMELL LOG.

Tomlinson almost chuckles. 'I'm supposed to fill that in each time I come down. For when they look over the building. Stupid.'

'What's it for?'

'It's a Smell Log,' he replies, in a tone of voice that suggests that should be self-explanatory. Then he adds grudgingly, 'You get some funny smells down here. Surveyor they had in reckoned rats are getting in somehow and dying underneath the floorboards, among the heating pipes. I'm supposed to keep a record if it starts to stink.'

The next room is piled high with office furniture; several desks like the one Tomlinson has in his room; hulks of metal cabinets; typists' chairs, some of which look as though they have never been used – the one nearest to Iris still has a triangular label attached to it. It says, *Flame Retardant Covers – Satisfaction Guaranteed*.

Tomlinson says, 'You should come down here some time and take a look round. Might be something you could use up in your office. Just going to waste down here. Some of it's quite new as well.'

'These desks are much nicer than the one I've got,' Iris says. 'God knows how you'd get one up to the third floor.'

The next room is smaller and also full of furniture. The one after that is smaller still and empty. It seems colder as well.

'There's some steps here,' says Tomlinson, 'mind how you go.'

They go through another door, heavily sprung, which slams shut behind them with a bang at the same time as Tomlinson flicks on a light. They are at the top of a short flight of steps which lead downwards into a long, low-ceilinged corridor. They are beneath the basement.

The corridor is lit with one old bulb which is directly above their heads, just inside the door. The quality of the light is different from the rooms they have just been in; less distinct, more yellow. There is a dense coldness. It *feels* underground. The walls of the corridor are made up of large blocks of stone which have been painted over but not plastered. At the bottom of the steps, Tomlinson pauses. 'This is where I was telling you about,' he says quietly. Almost involuntarily, Iris glances back. She can feel an odd, uncomfortable sensation at the base of her spine.

They walk a few paces down the corridor. The light behind them throws monstrous shadows on the wall. Then Iris hears a click and realises that Tomlinson has brought a torch. The illumination it provides is weak and watery. He passes a hollow, unconvincing beam along the left hand wall. 'See, there.'

Ranged along the length of the wall are four small cells, lined with brick, no more than five feet tall at their highest point and less than five feet deep.

'There's others further along,' Tomlinson says, 'but it's just more of the same. Do you want to take a look?'

'No,' Iris says, 'I don't.'

They stand in silence for a moment, the weight of history pressing down on them as large and as complex as the building above their heads. Iris thinks of all the contacts she can make with her computer, the sheer width of knowledge at her fingertips, and how it all seems at this moment to be futile and shallow, broadness without depth; for she cannot reach down in time to a person kept in one of those cells and say, *in a hundred years, somebody will stand here and think of you.*

'It's a woman,' Tomlinson says gently. 'The ghost. A woman. Probably a woman who died here, I would think.

Some say it is the pain that traps them in time, although I think that's a bit fanciful. Maybe she's nothing to do with the place. But I think so. I felt so, at the time.'

'In one of the cells?'

Tomlinson shakes his head. 'No, she was coming towards me here, along the corridor. She passed me, then just disappeared. She was small, and holding something in her arms. She was wearing a brown dress, down to her ankles. Her hair was short, shorn off. That's what made me think she was an inmate.'

'Were you frightened?' she asks.

'No,' he says. 'I was surprised, well while it was happening I was surprised but it only lasted a second. Then afterwards I felt not surprised at all, if you know what I mean.'

They stand in silence for a moment. Then Iris says, 'I think I'd like to go back up now.'

They turn and go back along the corridor, Tomlinson ahead because he is holding the torch. Iris stays close behind. They mount the steps and open the heavy door into the empty room, where Tomlinson gestures for her to go ahead so that he can turn lights off behind them as they go.

As they pass through the furniture Iris asks him over her shoulder, 'Did you say the dress was brown?'

'Yes.'

Getting back to the room of stacked shelving seems to take a long time. The cold white light of the fluorescent tubes seems positively cheery; the filthy box files seem like old friends.

They go back through the swing doors and without speaking begin to climb the flight of stairs which lead up to the ground-floor corridor, to Tomlinson's room and the front entrance, to the drone and mundanity of London mid-evening, midweek. At the top of the stairs, Tomlinson pauses by a bank of lights.

While she waits for him, Iris turns and glances back down the stairs. The wide, shallow steps and the smooth brass handrail plunge and fade. As Tomlinson clicks off each switch, a section of the stairwell is swallowed by darkness, beginning at the bottom and progressing up towards them.

Suddenly, she feels gripped with knowledge – and coldly determined.

Whatever you are, she thinks with fierce calm, *you're not getting me*.

7

What to wear to visit one's therapist is a major dilemma – and one for which the fashion industry has so far failed to produce an adequate response. On the whole, I favour basic black. They like you in black. It has all the obvious connotations, chief amongst them being funereal gloom (which pleases the old rapists no end) but it also renders you plain and blank, a *tabula rasa*, a blackboard – and blackboards are made to be scribbled on.

There are days, however, when black will not do. For one thing, it is a good idea to keep them guessing; constant gloom and you are nothing more than a good old-fashioned depressive and frankly, darling, they are ten-a-penny in the bonkers business. The occasional glimpse of a multiple personality keeps them on their toes. For that, you need a bit of variety.

This has always been fairly easy for me. Being self-employed I have a whole wardrobe full of guises: leggings and saggy jumpers on the days I am at home pretending to do my filing, business suits for formal meetings, trousers and trendy shirts for chats with casual contacts. My previous life, before Peter, was a sequence of self-revelatory decisions. Each morning, as I rolled out of bed with a soft, baby-monkey whimper, I would do two things: run my hands through my hair to make sure nothing had been nesting in it overnight, then wonder fuzzily, *now, who am I today?*

Today I have a thousand other sorts of choices to make, most of which are far more immediate. Yesterday was a pretty busy day, as far as epiphanies go. Yesterday, I looked myself in the face and failed to understand what I saw: but today I could sit down with pen, paper and a bit of imagination and try to work it out. That is what I ought to be doing.

Therapists think that you spend your whole life trying to come up with excuses not to see them. I have cancelled my last four visits (which I still have to pay for, incidentally). Today I do not cancel but I am taking the easy way out. Psychologically, I am shattered. I am going to see her as an excuse not to think about anything.

I throw a selection of items on the bed, instantly dismissing the ones she has already seen. From then on it is a process of elimination. Trim grey jacket? I am not in the mood to be a control freak with a pathological fear of commitment or dependency, not this morning anyway. Wacky red and orange dress? I am not sure I am up to mania either. Virginal white blouse twinned with large plastic crucifix? Nope. We did my potential schizoid tendencies back in January.

Aha. I have it. Slut.

Subtle slut, that is. Nothing as obvious as leather mini-skirt and fishnet stockings (try that one, baby, and you're right back to schizoid tendencies). No, this requires a little thought. It is essential to let them think they have figured it out for themselves. So, I settle on a white body made of soft cotton jersey that clings to my ribcage. Then I slide on jeans with a leather belt clasped by a huge chunky buckle that emphasises the fragility of my waspish waist. To this ensemble will be added my soft denim jacket, sky blue with the cuffs rolled up, along with black leather lace-up boots. My hair I pin upwards with combs and grips but being a little short for this malarky within minutes it is tumbling and whispering around my face, which is the whole point; eyeliner on the upper lid only, to give a wide-eyed look; pink blusher; rosebud lips. I have the thoughtful pout down to a fine art.

I practise anyway, in the oak-framed mirror which is propped up in the hallway. I jam my hands in the pockets of my jacket and scowl. I give a sphinx-like smile. I turn my head away and then glance back. The look is convincing, this morning. Sex bomb trying to be casual. Kitten on her day off. Come and get me, boys (of either gender).

It is all in the manner, of course. Clothes alone will not do it. It's attitude that counts. If I went to see my shrink dressed like this but with my shoulders drooping I would look ridiculous. The trick is to breeze in through the door, drop into the chair with an insouciance that would make Brigitte Bardot look dreary, slump back with a sigh and say, 'Morning, Doc. How are we today then?'

To this, my therapist gives a response which is no more reactive than a stare. I often think that one day I should arrive stark naked, just to make her eyelids flicker; but this lady is one cool customer. She would probably glance at me with that summarising, dismissive look which says that she has seen *that* trick three times this week and I am going to have to come up with something *far* more original if I expect to throw *her*.

This, to me, is one of the most oppressive things about being crackers: the constant desire to entertain my shrink. I am coming here to be turned into someone slightly normal after all, not Ken Dodd.

Today, however, I think I may be in with a chance of gaining the upper hand. It is clear as soon as our gazes meet that she is having an off day. Appearance-wise I have an unfair advantage. She doesn't have anything like my sartorial variety. She wears the solid, intelligent-but-caring woman's uniform of brightly coloured woollen cardigan and long, full skirt with ethnic zig-zag pattern. Her hair is drawn back into a matching cloth band. She wears no make-up and her earrings are constructed out of Genuine Wood.

She seems a bit on the pale side. I worry about her pallor. I worry that my appointment is at 12.10 which must be her last session before lunch. This means that she must always be hungry when she sees me, must always have her mind stretching towards the moment when she can lean forward and say gently, 'Well, it's time.'

I decide to try and liven up her day, take her mind off her stomach. I assume the pose, slumping down in the chair, foot up on one knee. It is something I can do easily with my long legs and it looks particularly good in jeans. It combines flirtatious indifference with a hint of androgyny.

I glance at the wall and, while I do so, knit my fingers together in my lap. Then I glance down at them. Then, swiftly, I give her a cool look and say, in a voice which is teasingly soft, 'I think it's time we talked about my promiscuity.'

As I drove back to Peter's house in the Mini, I thought about the history of mental illness in my family and wondered just how mental it was. It seems to have afflicted the women mostly. (Now there's a surprise.) It also seems to have gone hand in hand with the arrival of babies, one of the many reasons why I have always given childbirth a swerve. The stories have been passed down through the mothers who seem – thankfully – to have become less mad as the generations progressed.

My great-gran was the most undilutedly mad. My mother used to talk about her as the source of all our troubles, as if she was Eve. She was twenty-four when she gave birth to my gran and went neatly round the twist within weeks. She was committed to an asylum where the inmates were in the habit of sharing both their syphilis and their tuberculosis. She lasted less than a year.

Gran was raised by an uncle or aunt – the father not figuring in this story at all, apparently – and told my mother nearly every day of her childhood that she had no idea how lucky she was to have a mother at all. She told her this as she stood over her and watched her scrub floors, adding for good measure that she was an ugly little girl who was fit for little else. By all accounts, it was a pretty unpleasant upbringing. So I, in my turn, was told by *my* mother that I had no idea how lucky I was not to have a mother who constantly told me how lucky I was to have a mother at all. You can see why I don't want a child myself.

My mother never told me I was ugly but she cried frequently, which made me feel ugly inside. If I misbehaved she cried. If I disliked the latest frilly dress she had bought for me she cried. If I hid in a corner and read a book she sobbed her heart to pieces.

I grew up sullen and bewildered. According to my mum, my ignorance of what she had been through as a girl meant I was just plain selfish. This was no more than a refined twist on a conveniently inherited argument, although my mother would never have seen it that way. It is a child's job not to comprehend. If children comprehended what was in store for them in adulthood, it is doubtful whether they would bother to get up in the morning, Rice Krispies or no.

So it all came down to my Victorian great-gran, who was the most selfish of all because she had a baby and went mad.

After her, we had our girl babies late, perhaps trying to cram some life in before our brains gave out. My mother was born when Gran was forty-four. She was the ninth child, not counting two that didn't survive, but the first and only female. After her, Gran stopped, as if in my mother she had finally produced a fit repository for her woes.

My mother was thirty-nine when she had me but I was the first, not the last, and the only.

I have said that the mothers became less mad with each generation but as I turned the corner into Lake View I wondered out loud to myself if that was the case. The mothers stayed mad, I think, but the world around them changed. They were allowed their madness as an inevitable part of their condition. Perhaps it was almost expected of them. Perhaps these days it is marked down as a reward.

I parked the car and said to myself, 'I am not mad.'

The engine was still running. I was in neutral, with my head leaning forward on the wheel. I was looking at the house in front of me and thinking how long it was going to take to search from top to bottom and how I didn't want to do it. I was thinking how, up until now, I had not really taken control of what was happening to me but allowed other people to drop me small particles of information at whatever rate they pleased.

I can recommend thinking out loud to yourself in a parked Mini with the engine running. They are such low-slung, flimsy cars. They automatically induce a sense of inferiority and caution. You don't pick a fight with anybody when you're driving a Mini.

My vulnerability suddenly annoyed me. I sat up, put the car into reverse and began to back out of the drive. I had just remembered what my mad old great-gran was called. It had given me an idea.

'My great-gran was called Sophie.'

'Oh, really?'

'Or maybe it was Sophia. Did they have Sophie in those days? It sounds more modern to me.' I shrugged.

Sophie was wearing a blue dress and a panic-stricken expression. The dress was irritating me. It was one of those loose-waisted, little-girl styles with a long skirt in large pleats. If women went around in school uniforms people would point and laugh, yet there are whole clothing chainstores founded on the principle that it is a good idea to appeal to men's fantasies about toddlers.

I had arrived at a bad moment. The front door was open, as if Sophie was expecting someone else. I walked down the hallway and through the immaculate kitchen to the office, where Sophie was sitting at a long table piled high with sealed jiffy bags. The ones on her left were labelled. The pile on her right was waiting to be addressed. She had her head bent over the table and was consulting a list, pressing a ruler to it and glancing along, checking that something was right.

At the sound of my approach she flicked her head casually towards the doorway and almost did a double take when she saw it was me. 'Bet!' she said, a wide-eyed, big-toothed smile spreading over her uncertain face. 'Hi . . .

what a nice surprise. What brings you here? I thought we'd see you on Friday.'

I spread my hands. 'Oh, just popped in. Got a bit bored in the house, you know. Sorry, are you working?'

She rose from the chair and turned the list over, then waved both hands, ushering me backwards into the kitchen. 'No no of course not, let's have a drink. Great . . .'

She talked throughout the coffee-making process, about how she wasn't really busy, about how it was nothing important. It was wonderful to see me. It was lovely that I had dropped by unexpectedly. Really nice. I thought I saw her glancing towards the front door several times but I couldn't be sure. She was such a fluffy bunny it might have been a nervous tic.

'That's what made me think of popping over,' I said nonchalantly. 'I was thinking about my mum and my great-gran and trying to remember what her name was and I remembered it was Sophie, so I thought why don't I pop over and say hi.' I took a sip of coffee. 'I like your dress.'

'Thanks,' Sophie said distractedly. 'It's an old one. Alex likes it.'

I bet he does, I thought.

'Actually, Sophie . . .' I lowered my cup and looked down into it. We were both standing, leaning up against counters which were perpendicular to one another. Sophie had pointedly not asked me to sit down.

She recognised the interrogatory tone of my voice and looked at me in alarm. I had her attention, finally .

'Actually, well to be perfectly honest, seeing as I've got

you alone. There's some things I wanted to ask you, about Peter. I wouldn't really want to ask when Alex was around. It's not that kind of thing.'

'About the company?' She was so worried she wasn't even listening to me properly.

'No, not the company, I know to ask Alex about that and it's still fine and everything. No, about Peter.'

She looked slightly relieved but still apprehensive. Her tone was guarded. 'Go on.'

There is a trick I learnt at school about getting into fights. You get your opponent to drop their guard by turning as if you are going to walk away. Instead, you gain momentum for your swing. I had just pulled the verbal equivalent on Sophie.

'Who is Iris?'

She nearly dropped her coffee on her pristine marbled linoleum. I was making a habit out of surprising other women in their kitchens.

'Why?' she said, floundering. 'Why do you want to know? What . . .'

'I found something,' I said, 'in the dining-room, in the sideboard. I found a letter. It was a love letter, from someone called Iris. Well I say a love letter but actually it was pretty venomous. It was clear they had had something going and it was all over. I couldn't work out the details. The postmark was faded so I don't know whether it was recent or not. Maybe she was a girlfriend from way back but it didn't look that old.' I decided to appeal to what little sense of female solidarity Sophie might possess. 'I know it's really awful to ask you this, to spring this on you, but I really need to know . . . was Peter faithful to me?'

She smiled and exhaled. 'Oh Bet, he was bananas about you . . . please, you musn't think . . .'

To my surprise, a tear had sprung to my eye. I even managed a sniffle. 'Well who was she then?'

There was a kitchen chair at the corner of the nearby table. Sophie sank diagonally into it. 'Oh God, sit down.'

I sat on a chair on the other side of the corner.

Sophie launched straight in. At first I thought that she was still in a hurry, anxious to get this little chat over with before her visitor arrived, but as she warmed to her topic I realised there was more to it than that. Soft little Sophie was doing something which I would not have thought her capable of. She was being bitchy.

'This is all ancient history you know, really, I can't believe we're talking about that woman. The problem with Iris was she was a real martyr, you know the type. Iris was going to spend her whole life being victimised by somebody. She and Peter were *completely* unsuited. I can't think what he saw in her. Well, I suppose she was quite pretty, although she could have done something about her hair I think.' Sophie sighed. 'Some girls, you know, you just feel they're asking for it. Peter had had a lot of girlfriends. Well, you know that already. He got about a bit. Like a hot knife through butter, as Alex puts it. Girls like Iris seemed to like it. They met at a party we had here. She knows someone we know. I think they went straight back to his place.' She pulled a face. 'It didn't last very long,' she continued, 'well we knew it wouldn't. She didn't like us much either. Probably thought we were a bad influence.'

Oh really, I thought, *I wonder why.*

'After Peter finished with her it all went a bit sour. She got hysterical. Ringing him up in the middle of the night. She went a bit mad. She even rang here once at five o'clock in the morning, accusing us of all sorts, turning him against her. Completely mad. Alex told her where to go in no uncertain terms. I couldn't believe it when she turned up at the funeral.'

I remembered my promise to Iris. 'Oh,' I said, 'which one was she?'

Sophie shook her head. 'You probably won't remember. Too much make-up. Hair all over the place. She's going to look dreadful when she's forty – the kind of woman who tries too hard. Desperate for a man, that's her problem. Well there does seem to be a bit of shortage these days. But some women only have themselves to blame, in my opinion. They think they can have it both ways . . .'

I was very, very anxious not to hear Sophie's opinions on feminism, which I felt would be sadly predictable. Her jiffy bags were forgotten; her imminent visitor forgotten. She was about to tell me how much she liked being married, even though she and Alex had their ups and downs, and that she didn't have any problem with changing her name to his and couldn't understand women who did.

'I knew when I got married that some things would have to go,' she began, 'but I didn't have a problem with that. We had a lovely wedding.'

145

I rose to my feet. She looked up at me, momentarily bewildered. She had just settled in for a nice girly chat, after all.

'Oh,' she said, coyly, pressing her lips together in a sympathetic grimace. 'I'm sorry. I suppose it must be quite difficult for you, now Peter is gone.'

I was cold with fury. Did this powdered little dolly really imagine that I envied *her*? 'You're busy . . .' I said lamely. 'I shouldn't really keep you talking.'

She rose too. I picked up both of our coffee cups and turned to the sink, swilling them with water before putting them down.

As I shrugged my denim jacket back on, I asked her, 'Oh, one other thing. What does a bond look like? I've never seen one.'

Her face was blank. She knitted her brow, questioning.

'A bond, you know. A share certificate,' I insisted.

Sophie's problem was not just stupidity. She couldn't even remember the story they had told me. It was several seconds before light dawned. 'Oh the company thingies, the papers. Um. I don't know. I never saw them. Alex knows.'

One of the cuffs of my jacket had come unrolled. I turned it back up, fiddling with the stud button. 'Oh well,' I said lightly. 'I suppose Alex can tell me when you come over on Friday.'

When I looked up she was nodding a lot.

As I pulled out of their drive, Alex pulled in, at the wheel of a dirty green transit van. I waved cheerily and Alex lifted a hand.

I drove home wondering what the plan was, how Sophie was supposed to distract me while Alex found whatever it was they were really looking for. Perhaps she was going to fake a period pain so that she and I could retire to the bathroom and discuss feminine hygiene, along with how essential it was to use a lash-separating comb when you applied mascara.

As I drove down Lake View for the second time that day, I noticed something odd about the over-priced dwellings that lined each side of the road; too tightly packed to be secluded homes, too large to form a community.

All the windows were different. Some were mullioned. Some were bay. Some were double-glazed with sliding partitions. One was semi-circular and rose the entire length of the house. The street was a glazier's heaven.

At the end of Lake View was a large pond called The Basin, with ducks and geese huddled together around its uncertain, twig-clogged edges. I drove past it then back again. Its surface was a slash of gold in the glimmering, afternoon light. The windows of the Lake View houses were like that pond: reflecting everything, revealing nothing. They were designed to be seen rather than looked into. They were statements in their own right, not means to an end.

I swerved into Peter's drive a little too fast, braked and stalled. I was parked skew-whiff but pulled the handbrake on anyway, knowing that if I started the engine again there was a possibility I would back out of the drive and never come back.

Peter's windows were ordinary, casement, unflashy. Peter's house did not draw attention to itself. As I thought this, for the first time, I began to fear what I might find inside.

Inside the front door, I paused and listened. Very little traffic noise percolated down this road. There was the singular chirrup of a blackbird.

I am not mad.

I tossed the car keys on the hallway table and picked up the phone, fumbling in my jacket pocket for the piece of paper which I thought would have Iris's number. My fingers discovered it and fumbled to unwrap it, while the other hand still held the telephone receiver to my ear. I withdrew the paper and frowned at it. In pencil, scrawled, were her address and some directions. That was all.

The dialling-tone buzzed uselessly in my ear. I dropped the receiver back into place, scowling. I wanted to ring Iris to warn her I had mentioned her to Sophie and reassure her I hadn't broken my promise, just in case they rang her. I didn't even know her second name.

I checked my watch. It was still early. I could drive over. But then she had said she would ring. Perhaps I should leave it up to her. I had a feeling that Iris was only a bit-part in all this, a ghost which Sophie and Alex would rather disappeared in a puff of smoke. I didn't think she would be much good in a crisis and I wasn't inclined to try and make an ally of her. She seemed to have too much to lose.

It was midnight by the time I got to bed – and I was beginning to feel that I might have inherited more from my great-gran than I had previously realised. Spending too much time in a house is like living inside your own head. Each room becomes a function of yourself, a physical expression of all the nasty little corners tucked and turned in the interior of your cranium.

The story I had made up about the letter from Iris sent me straight to the sideboard in the sitting-room, which contained nothing more than some rather upsetting dining paraphernalia – prize for the most tasteless *objet* going to a large, laminated table mat with a watercolour picture of a volcano surrounded by forest. Landscapes always make me shudder. They are so empty.

The downstairs of the house yielded little in the way of oddities. At the back of the kitchen, there was a pantry, small, with a sliding door, shelved and whitewashed inside. It was mostly tins: beans, soup, fruit salad – and packets of various practical supplies. Peter clearly had a neurosis about running out of kitchen roll. I lifted the lids of a few cardboard boxes and discovered one which was full of eggs, now past their *Best Before* date by over a fortnight. *Don't most people keep eggs in the fridge these days?* Next to the eggs was a smaller cardboard box which contained six bottles of baby oil.

Upstairs, I hovered briefly on the landing. I had been

through the bedroom before, looking for places to put my own things, shirts to borrow. It didn't feel like new territory, and anyway, I had been going to bed in there every night. It was hard to believe that I had been sleeping with secrets. But I had to try, at least, to be thorough. As I pulled the clothes out of the wardrobe I reflected that it was something I would have had to do sooner or later. I tossed the suits to one side. They wouldn't fit anyone I knew. Alex was too short and stocky. They could go to a charity shop or something.

I sat on the floor to pull out the shoes. That was how I noticed the other slightly unusual thing – a stick at the back of the wardrobe, a plain wooden pole propped up in the corner. I pushed some of the shoes clear so that I could look at it. I pulled a face. It looked like something ordinary.

The shoes were heaped on the carpet in front of me, ten or twelve of them in a jumbled pile. I sat with my legs either side of them, like a child playing with seashells on the beach. Idly, I began to sort them into pairs. It was as I picked up the black leather brogues that I began to feel sad, diminished. Peter had worn these a lot. I turned them over. They still looked quite new. I rubbed at a scuff of chalky dirt on one toe, then slipped my hands inside the shoes, one in each, feeling the slight springiness of the soles, the weight of them.

There are some things which are undeniably male, and one of these is shoes. Shirts, jackets, trousers – these things are not mysterious to me – but Peter's shoes were so solid, so unlike my own, so *other*. I felt the exact shape and size of what I had lost. I remembered the tendons on his toes.

I closed my eyes in pain. His feet were as clear to me as if I had seen them an hour ago – but for the life of me I could not remember his face.

I put the radio on as I was getting ready for bed. It felt suddenly important to have some noise. While I sat on the side of the bed and peeled off my jeans, I listened to a news item about European currency exchange rates and the black economy. I thought how odd it was that the small rectangle by Peter's bedside – no bigger than a box of tissues – could contain such a wealth of information. Inside that box was the world but the box was inside this bedroom and the bedroom inside the house: so could the world also exist outside this house?

It was all gone. I was marooned here, free-floating in the universe.

As I fell asleep I thought about the scene at the beginning of *The Wizard of Oz*, where the tornado comes to Kansas, lifts the little wooden homestead clean off its foundations and sends it whirling up into the air with Dorothy and Toto inside. *Was the dog called Toto?* Lucky Dorothy, I thought dreamily, at least she had a dog. What did I have? Well, there was Benby . . . he was the nearest I was going to get to a small, helpful animal, with the emphasis on *small*.

I dreamed of Toto, who worked in an office in central London. I dreamed that I opened the door of his office and found my mother cooking an omelette. She turned and gave me a malevolent smile. I ran on the spot until she melted away. Then suddenly, out of the white air, the wall of a huge stone building rushed towards me. A small man with cake crumbs on his lower lip stood at the side and laughed. The building hit me bang in the face and I woke up.

It was morning. I was sitting half-upright, propped up on one elbow. I blinked. It was morning. But I felt as though I had been asleep for only minutes. Pictures from my dream rushed through my head. I closed my eyes and lay back on my pillow, raising my hands to push the moistly affectionate duvet down, away from my chest. Then I spreadeagled my arms on either side of my body, splayed out in a starfish pose, trying to cool off.

The sense of the dream was with me and I lay waiting for it to evaporate. When it didn't, I struggled out a hand and hit the radio alarm. The on-the-hour news leapt into the bedroom. It was the same item about the black economy that I had been listening too as I had undressed the previous night. I hit the button again and the world vanished. The feeling was still there, as if I was a chameleon and my skin had changed colour during my dream. I would have to wait a few minutes for it to wear off, for me to change back into being who I really was; awake, alive. In the meantime, I thought about how everybody in my dream – Benby,

Toto, my mother, the little man – were all saying the same thing. They were all trying to tell me that I didn't exist.

8

All along, something had bothered me about Benby. I had thought that what was bothering me was that he was a slimy git. But now I knew that I was wrong. In my effort to acknowledge the obvious, I had overlooked the detail. I had relied on instinct and the instinct had been right: yes, Benby was a slimy git. But he was a slimy git with a strong sense of propriety, a slimy git who chose his words carefully and never said one thing when he meant something else.

Turn to page one. That is what I had always said to myself in the past when I was trying to work something out and it had never failed me. On page one of my story, Benby had called me into his office and informed me that one week before his death, Peter had altered his will, making me the sole beneficiary. Later in the conversation, I had asked if he thought it was odd, Peter dying so soon afterwards.

He had shrugged, then given a small tight smile. 'You would be surprised how often it happens,' he had said – and logically, I suppose it must. Let's say X out of ten people make their wills each week, and Y out of ten die each week. The probability of somebody dying within a week of making their will is X divided by ten times Y divided by ten; a fraction, but then there are a lot of people in the world. Sometimes murderers get caught because they are AB Rhesus negative, which appears in less than half of one per cent of the population. Come the trial, the defence counsel stands up in court and points out that in a city of eight million inhabitants, thirty-six thousand of them will have that blood group. It doesn't mean that thirty-six thousand people were picked up by the police two miles down the road carrying a machete dripping with blood and laughing maniacally but nobody thinks of that. Thirty-six thousand. Could have been any one of them. Not guilty, m'lud.

Perhaps people become accident-prone after making their wills. Knowledge can make you careless, reckless even. We have all done it on a lesser scale. We have all reached out for the wine glass sitting upturned on the kitchen shelf and thought – that glass is going to slip from my fingers, drop to the floor and smash. Our hand has gone into slow motion. There is plenty of time to think, yet never enough to stop our hand from reaching out.

Perhaps it is even simpler than that. Perhaps, when you have made a will, a very small part of you gives up. You have not just accepted your own mortality, you have written down that you accept your own mortality and signed it in front of witnesses. Everyone will know, forever, that on that day you decided to die.

Maybe everything that happens after that is a postscript and the ties that bind loosen in a way which is so tiny and obscure as to be almost imperceptible – but vital nonetheless. Then, if the time comes unexpectedly, you do not shriek and rage quite as loudly as you might have done because, in your heart of hearts, you have already said goodbye.

All this time, I thought to myself, shaking my head at my own lack of insight, *all this time I have been so hung up on Peter dying just after visiting Benby that I have never really thought of it as him visiting Benby just before he died*. I had been so distracted by the fact that there was no apparent causal link going forwards, that it had never occurred to me that there might just be a backwards one. Peter did not know he was going to die. But he might have known that he might. A car crash got him. But he could have been expecting something else.

It had been staring me in the face – or, rather, blaring me in the ear. I had gone back over my first meeting with Benby time and time again and missed it each time, like a woman looking for a contact lens in a field of grass, seeing nothing but green. Benby never said one thing when he meant another. A week before his death, Peter had visited him and altered his will, naming me as the sole beneficiary.

He didn't make a will. He altered it.

If you ever wish to hide a fact from anyone, then hide it in their ego. The one thing I had not asked myself, at any point, was the one thing on everybody else's mind. Why me?

I had been looking in the mirror and thinking that the answer was obvious. Now it was time to reflect.

Every word means at least one thing but some mean a lot more. The word *alsike*, for instance, means a species of Swedish clover. You can say alsike in as many different ways as you like. You can say it sincerely. You can say it sarcastically. You can shout from the rooftops of the House of Commons while pointing at a naked Tory MP that you have strapped to a chimney pot. All it will mean is that you are accusing him or her of being a form of Scandinavian undergrowth.

On the whole, your acting talents are wasted on nouns.

The word *along*, however, is a different matter. Along generally means joining up with but can also mean lengthwise, from end to end, following, through the length of (in which case you would be wise to avoid confusion and stick to the somewhat old-fashioned *alongst*), on account of, depending, belonging and so on. Once you bung in a bit of irony you can take it almost anywhere.

The word *alter* usually means to make otherwise or different in some respect, without changing the thing itself. Strictly speaking, an altered will is not one which is torn up and rewritten completely but one where a lawyer takes his mental Tippex to the name JONES and changes it to SMITH. His is not to reason why.

Benby was unimpressed by my grasp of grammar, which made me wonder whether I should have tried physical violence instead.

He gave a weary sigh, then pursed his lips. We were in his office. I had arrived without an appointment but he knew better than to get his secretary to throw me out. He leant forward over his desk and put both elbows on the table, then rested his face in his hands with the palms pressing either cheek, distorting his features. He remained in this position for some time, staring at me glumly.

'Why are you smiling?' he mumbled eventually.

'Because you look like Deputy Dawg.'

It was like the sun coming out. Suddenly, unexpectedly, his face cracked open and he gave a huge, responsive smile, rueful but uncontrollable. I knew that at that moment that I had broken through. He was finally going to crawl out of his own backside and give me some useful information.

He leant back in his padded chair and hooked both hands behind his head, like an American attorney. The two sides of his shirt parted company and I was treated to a quick glimpse of pale belly.

'Felicity,' he said – no, groaned. 'What I am about to tell you is, strictly speaking, a sort of professional misconduct. A client remains a client even when they are dead.' He was massaging his closed eyes with one set of fingers. I waited for him to deal with his ethical difficulties in his own way. After a pause he leant forward again, returning to his original position. 'Although it's true I didn't receive any clear guidance from Mr Attwell about information that you were or were not to be given, not surprisingly I suppose, as he had no idea he was about to die in a road accident.' He raised both hands, palms upwards, then dropped them into his lap.

The body language was all very impressive – reluctance, I was getting the point – but I was still waiting for hard information.

'The original will,' Benby said slowly, 'was made out to a Mr and Mrs Littleton. Friends of the deceased, I believe, but Mr Attwell said something about a business arrangement, which is why I had to investigate if he owned anything beyond what I knew about already – did you know that solicitors have a legal obligation to be nosy these days? New regulations. Two years ago. Anyway I got the impression when the will was first drawn up, last year, that it was some sort of reciprocal arrangement, as if he might be paying off a debt of some sort, or maybe just trying to reassure them, I don't know.'

'When he came in here to alter it, did you ask him why?'

Benby spread his hands again. 'Not my job, as his solicitor . . . not my job.'

'How about as a human being?'

'As a human being, I would have said he was upset with them in some way. He seemed agitated when he first arrived. By the time he left he seemed to have cheered up, as if it was all some kind of in-house joke.'

I exhaled, a long deep sigh, allowing myself to sink into my chair. Peter got his will altered in my favour as a joke? A malicious surprise for a couple of people he had fallen out with? 'So,' I said, 'you're saying you don't think he altered the will because he wanted to leave everything to me, he altered it because he wanted it kept out of the hands of the Littletons, on the off-chance anything happened to him.'

Benby pushed out his chin and gave a small nod of agreement. 'That was the impression he gave – but then I didn't ask him any questions about you.'

'So, it was spite, not because he ... not because he particularly wanted it to go to me.'

Benby gave me a long, sympathetic gaze. Then he said gently, 'He could have left it to Battersea Dogs Home, you know.'

I looked at the floor. I knew I sounded spoilt but I couldn't help it. 'Might have saved me a lot of trouble if he had.'

'He clearly thought you could cope.'

Our gazes met and I knew that we were both thinking the same thing. It was much more likely, in fact, that Peter didn't think I would ever have to cope. Peter didn't know about the lorry and the van and the side road on the Watford by-pass.

I wondered where the lorry was when Peter was altering his will. Perhaps, as he was bending to sign, it was thundering along a motorway somewhere and the driver was whistling and thinking vaguely that maybe, sometime soon, he ought to have his tyres checked. Where was I? I struggled to locate myself in this scenario; as if it made any difference what position the world was in at that particular moment; as if I could freeze everything at that point and just take a look around, like a visitor to Madame Tussaud's; as if it mattered.

I rose to my feet, crossed my arms and wandered over

to the window. The view was uninspiring; roofs below and shapes of neighbouring buildings, a series of flat and perpendicular perspectives in uninventive browns, like empty boxes. Looking out of that window and the dim sky beyond, it was possible to believe that some virus had struck the city and it was deserted, that Benby and I were the only living things left on the planet.

'Did the police find anything?' I asked wearily, without turning around.

'No . . .' Benby said. 'But I didn't request a comprehensive search, just his papers. I could have taken it further but I've done what I had to do, tried to find out. Legally, I think I've discharged my responsibilities.'

I turned back from the window. 'Well,' I said, as I walked back over to my chair. 'If I find anything then I'll let you know.'

I meant it, and Benby knew I meant it. He gestured with his hands, 'I'd be grateful . . .'

'Goodbye,' I said, crossing to the door.

I turned back as I left. The glance he gave me was benign, almost paternal. 'Goodbye.'

By the time I got home it was getting dark; early, even for March – but it felt more as though it had never really got light. The streets were quieter than usual, even the trees seemed grey and lifeless. Driving down Lake View I saw not one single soul. It was a moonscape.

I made myself a cup of coffee and a cheese sandwich, then sat looking at the sandwich while I drank the coffee.

I felt as though I had wasted the week, even though I knew I hadn't. It was Thursday and the next day Sophie and Alex were coming over. Anything else that I wanted to do in the house had to be sorted out that night.

I had done the garage, the kitchen, the study, the spare room and the sitting-room. The bedroom didn't have anything else in it to do. Short of dismantling the plumbing, there was nothing to be done in the bathroom or the downstairs toilet either.

I stared at the sandwich, which seemed to have a greasy, unhelpful quality, squatting there on its plate.

There was no escaping it. It was time to search the attic.

The entrance to the attic was in the ceiling of the landing, outside the main bedroom and just beyond the top of the oatmeal-carpeted stairs. It was a wooden square, painted the same colour as the ceiling, with a shallow rim. There was no handle or visible means of opening it. Unless you were looking specifically, you wouldn't even notice it was there.

I wasted a good half-hour looking for the stepladder which, I reasoned, ought to be within easy access. I had heard Peter going up into the attic, once, when I was making a phone call in the study. I had heard the shuffle of the wooden door and then the disembodied clump of his feet above my head. I was sure he had not gone out to the garage or the garden to get a ladder. I would have remembered that.

It got to the point where I was looking in idiotic places which were far too small to hold a ladder: the alcove underneath the shelving in the sitting-room, behind the door of the toilet. Then I remembered the stick in the wardrobe.

It was where I had left it, leaning in the corner.

Back on the landing, I reached up with the full length of my arms and pushed at the wooden square, which lifted upwards with ease. Using the blunt end of the stick, I manoeuvred the door to one side. A dark triangle appeared in the white wood and then sprouted edges, like a child's puzzle, became a polygon. When the door was finally edged out of the way it was a square again, this time of infinite, unfathomable black.

I brought the stick back down and turned it around. There was a shiny chrome hook on the other end. I pushed it up into the black square. It took a few minutes of fishing before it found the ladder, a lightweight metal one, specially balanced so that it flipped down out of the hole and unslid itself to the floor. I clambered up it unsteadily, still holding the stick in my left hand.

When my head and shoulders were in the attic I stopped and closed my eyes, to shut out the light from the hallway and let them adjust to the gloom. When I opened them again, I could see that the attic was huge, running almost the full length of the house, and that it had been partially converted. In front of me, the beams had been covered with boards on top of which a roll of beige carpet had been laid. Close to me, the carpet was tatty and wrinkled, but then it seemed to smooth out and sweep towards the far end of the attic where it disappeared beneath a pale grey hump which I could only see indistinctly.

I turned gingerly around on the metal stepladder. There was less light at the other end – my body blocked most of it out – but I could just make out what I was hoping to see, a pale thread of string which looped under the eaves. I reached out with the hooked end of the stick and tugged at it.

There was a click and ping and the attic was filled with thin, off-white light. A single bulb hung from a plastic-covered wire from which a few spiders' webs dangled redundantly, as if they had been hung out to dry. That end was more conventional, more what you would expect in an attic: bare beams wedged with fat fluffy layers of insulation felt, cardboard boxes, black plastic dustbin liners sealed with tape.

When I turned back round I could see that the other end was different. I clambered up the last few steps, onto the carpet.

The ceiling was higher than in most attics. I was in the middle and could stand up straight but could have moved much closer to the eaves before I would have had to bend. This end of the attic had been painted and plastered, not very well as far as I could tell, but at a glance it would almost pass for a usable room. The low grey hulk I had seen in the gloom was an unrolled sofa-bed or futon, on which there was a large, bulbous duvet with the sort of floral cover that you might get in the sales of a cut-price department store. Hanging above it, on the flat end wall, was a picture in a thin pine frame, a Chinese print of flowers. The only other furniture was a small, Formica chest of drawers.

For a guest bedroom, it was pretty sparse.

I turned to the other end of the attic and picked my way across the beams to the bags and boxes. They had been placed on a few pieces of rough hardboard and there was just enough space, underneath the light bulb, to kneel.

I pulled the nearest bag towards me.

Its contents were soft and pliable – its shape collapsed as I dragged it nearer with one arm. The tape was wrapped around the top and was old and stiff and unsticky. It unwound easily. Carefully, I peeled back the open plastic mouth.

Inside were clothes. A few flopped towards me. I pushed a hand in and rummaged around. There was a white cotton apron, something that looked and felt like a black dress in cheap polyester, a woman's blouse, a short pleated skirt, a pair of men's slacks in rabbit-dropping brown. It just looked like jumble.

I pushed it to one side, reached out a hand and squeezed two of the other bags. Same sort of feeling. I turned my attentions to the boxes.

There was a small one on top which I lifted down and placed on top of the bag I had opened. It was unsealed. I flipped open the cardboard lids and looked in: videos, blank by the look of them, some of them still sealed in their three-packs. Then, as I sat back on my heels, I saw a tall dark shape in the corner. In the second that it took my eyes to focus, my heart gave a tiny gulp of apprehension. Then I realised what it was – a camera tripod.

It was beginning to make sense but I needed more. I wanted something solid for my imagination to take hold of, something that said, you may think as many unpleasant things as you like and not feel guilty. It is all quite justified. You are not mad.

I found it in a low flat box which was stuck at the bottom of all the others. I singled it out because of its unusual shape. Getting to it required that everything else be moved to one side, which took some time.

The box was made of that thick, strong cardboard which is so tough it is almost wood and held together with industrial staples. The lid was a firm fit and I prised it off with difficulty. Inside there were sheaves of papers along with a scattering of diskettes in envelopes. I lifted those out and put them to one side. The first sheaf of paper was held together with a bulldog clip. I thought vaguely, *bulldog clip?* Didn't most people use paperclips these days?

It was a computer-generated list of names and addresses, the product of a cheap dot-matrix printer. About half of the addresses were in London but the rest were in various other parts of the country: Exeter, Dunstable, Market Harborough, Walton-on-Thames. The sheaf was several pages thick and the lines single-spaced. There were possibly hundreds of names. Then I saw that at the top of the first sheet someone had handwritten in capitals, HOLLAND. The next sheaf in the box was similar but headed GERMANY.

I pushed through the other bits and pieces: receipts, a roll of sticky labels, a few loose staples and drawing pins.

At the bottom of the box there was a fat, tatty A4 envelope, unsealed. I pulled it out and slid the contents onto my lap.

It was a wad of large, black and white prints, home-developed on old photographic paper with a white border. I lifted the pile up and scanned the top picture.

My brain must have become a little overloaded by that stage. There was so much in the picture that it took me several seconds to ingest the most important pieces of information. I absorbed them in reverse order.

There were three people, two men and one woman. The woman was centre stage and draped in a disarray of lingerie. Her head was thrown back. One of the men was at her side, crouched, licking her stomach. The other was behind her, with one arm descending to grasp a plump right breast and the other hand resting on the opposite shoulder.

After a moment's shock, I laughed out loud. The woman was Sophie. The men were Peter and Alex.

There were ten or so more photographs underneath. They appeared to show the sequence of the encounter. Sophie's underwear became progressively more distressed, the men's demands more inventive – although they never touched each other. The final shot was a Sophie sandwich, in which she was squeezed vertically between the two men while bits of her spilled out on either side. Her face was turned towards the camera and she looked as if she was wincing, more in irritation than in pleasure, as if she had just discovered a pebble in her shoe.

Early work. Before the technology improved. Before it progressed to video cameras and full colour, to movement and egg white mixed with baby oil. Before Peter cottoned on that there was a bit of money to be made.

Before he lost interest in doing his own dirty work.

It must have taken me nearly an hour after that but nothing else I found surprised me. One of the other boxes contained video equipment, including a hand-held camera which almost fitted my palm. I couldn't believe that something so tiny could be used for videoing anything bigger than a flower waving in the breeze. In one of the boxes there was a pile of magazines. You can guess their subject matter.

One of the black plastic bags contained a collection of those very thin, crackly bags that they give out free in supermarkets, the ones that break as you lift the food out of the car. Most of them were Sainsbury's. There were a couple of Tesco's. Inside the first there was a collection of underwear, all of it strappy. There were several suspender belts in different colours, knickers which were no more than bits of string – most of them black – and a pink bra with holes for the nipples, which I lifted out because I had never seen one before, shaking my head in wonder. It was made up of a cobweb of translucent lace and at the point where the straps met between the two cups were sewn six tiny pearl buttons in a flower arrangement.

As I turned it over, I saw that the back straps were grimy with dirt. Looking closer, I realised it was one of the grubbiest bras I had ever seen. It had probably never been washed.

For the first time, I began to feel sick.

My knees were hurting. I sat back on my bottom with my discoveries scattered over the boards. I cast my eye over the incongruous mix of items laid out before me: suspender belts, computer disks. I knew that I should be feeling shocked, upset – but actually, what I was feeling was disappointed.

So this is it, I thought. This is what Peter was into: nothing difficult or glamorous or dangerous, just ordinary smut, casual harm. He probably wasn't even very good at it. I sighed. I was trying not to take it to heart but his lack of imagination felt like a personal affront. Readers' wives? It was so suburban.

I have no idea how long I sat in the attic. My brain had lost all sense of time and eventually it was my stiffening body that told me it was late. I leaned forward to gather up the photographs and papers and put them back in the box.

It was then that I heard the noise.

There is something very odd that happens to a human body when it hears a sound which it knows is very bad news. It is a kind of freezing, a sensation which means a great deal more than becoming still. It is like an electrical charge – I felt it at that moment in my arms – a quivering, halfway between a shiver and a chill. At the same instant, there was a closing in of the hollowness inside my stomach.

It is a feeling peculiar to the only simple emotion human beings feel – fear. It is the sensation of the human body becoming animal. I have felt it only one or two times in my entire life. I felt it once when I got lost, on holiday at the age of twelve, and it grew dark, and just ahead of me on a deserted country lane there came the low growl of a dog.

I felt it when I answered the phone a week after my mother had been admitted to a cancer hospice and a sorrowful, sympathetic nurse's voice said, 'Miss Walker?'

I felt it then, in Peter's attic, as from the house below there came the unmistakable sound of somebody on the stairs.

I had noticed only the previous day that one of the stairs creaked – something you don't expect in a modern home. It was second from the top. It only creaked when you were coming up.

9

'D o you believe in ghosts?' Iris asks George, and Jerry squeals and giggles.

They are in Bottles Wine Bar. It is lunchtime. Iris was looking at the earrings in Next on High Holborn when she spotted the two of them by a stand near the door. The sight of George in a women's clothing shop was something to be seen. Jerry was holding a jumper up against herself, displaying it to him. George had been standing with his arms crossed, nodding, looking desperately interested.

Now they are in the wine bar round the corner: George's suggestion. He has bought a bottle of semi-expensive white. Iris has never seen him drink wine before, except at dinner.

She has thrown the question out light-heartedly, just to see what bites. She is not about to explain the whole escapade to them but wants to see how they will react. She is curious to know if what they say will make her instinctively side with Tomlinson, his practicality, his lack of romance or self-delusion on the topic.

Jerry is the kind of woman who squirms. She has dark,

curly hair and a tiny, turned-up nose. She is very, very pretty and Iris is trying hard not to hold this against her.

'My aunt saw a ghost once,' Jerry says. She has an upper-middle-class accent and a way of rushing her consonants together that suggests she is trying to sound not quite so upper-middle-class. Iris has no hesitation in holding that against her at all.

'It was my uncle,' Jerry continues, 'he appeared in her bedroom in the middle of the night and picked up a book and started reading. She was ever so shocked. He'd never read a book in his life.'

Iris wonders whether to expound Hart's *Six Theories about Apparitions*, then thinks better of it.

'Why do you ask?' asks George.

So far, he has hardly spoken to Iris. He has been observing Jerry with all the anxiety of a parent watching a child perform in the school play: and when he has spoken, his voice has been louder than usual and contained a note of false joviality.

'Our building is haunted, apparently,' Iris says. 'The porter told me about it. It's built on the foundations of a Victorian lunatic asylum. There's a woman in a brown dress who wanders around the basement. I thought maybe I would go down and explore.'

'Oh . . .' shivers Jerry, 'rather you than me.'

George is looking at Iris and she can tell that she has caught his attention. He is thinking of her fainting fit in the Cittie of Yorke. She feels pleased that, however momentarily, he must be wishing that Jerry

172

was not there, so that they could discuss it in more detail.

Jerry looks at her watch, which has a very thin, dark green, lizard-skin strap. 'We ought to be getting back soon, Georgie.'

'Yes, yes of course,' George booms. 'Right. Just go to the loo. Won't be a sec.'

Iris's wine glass is still full. She takes an ostentatiously large gulp from it.

'Oh sorry,' says Jerry in a rush, 'you haven't finished.'

Iris shrugs. There is a small pause. She wonders if she should take pity on Jerry and start asking all sorts of idiotic questions about how she and George first got talking over the photocopier.

'I went on a ghost hunt once,' Jerry says, and Iris looks at her in surprise. Now that George has gone, Jerry has stopped squirming. Even her accent sounds more natural.

'I was staying with some friends in a cottage in Suffolk. Their neighbour kept chickens, he was a policeman, and we went next door to borrow an egg. His wife worked in a pub near a church that was haunted. On the second of May every year it was supposed to walk in the churchyard at the stroke of twelve. It was the devil, a skeleton in a hooded cloak, who came back to get some money he was owed by a parishioner or something. The church was a couple of miles from the nearest village.' She finishes off her wine. 'We all went down on bikes and had a drink then left the bikes at the pub and walked down this track. It was pitch black of course but quite starry and misty, just the sort of night you would expect a ghost to turn up. Well I was completely petrified. Five minutes in this bloody graveyard, I thought, then I'm off. I kept pretending I was cold so that I would have an excuse to insist we all left.'

Iris has forgotten her wine. 'What happened?'

'We got halfway down the track, we could see the church against the sky. Then we saw lights behind us. It was a car. Actually, it was about four cars. They reached us just as we got to the church gate.' She begins to laugh. 'It was like Clapham Junction! I thought we were going to be standing in this deserted graveyard in the dark, you've never seen anything like it. Teenagers got out of the cars, all the local lads with cans of beer, and their girlfriends pretending to be scared. Then when we got into the graveyard there were even more people. There was one man wearing headphones and holding something that looked like a divining rod. There were four people in duffel coats with a video camera, a local reporter. It was amazing. The serious ghost hunters were not at all happy with the teenagers, of course, tramping all over the place and waving their torches. Then a group of Satanists arrived in long cloaks, lit candles and stood round in a circle going *ohm* . . .' They both laughed. 'It was pure Alan Ayckbourn.'

'What was?' George has reappeared. He looks pleased at the sight of Jerry and Iris enjoying a joke together.

Jerry simpers. 'Oh it's a long story, I'll tell you later. Just silly really.'

George is standing next to Jerry. He looks down at her.

Then he reaches out with a hand and, very softly, touches her cheek.

Just that; nothing more definite, nothing more possessive, just the lightest of touches, as if he wants to reassure himself that she is corporeal, that his hand will not pass through her like mist. She smiles up at him.

Iris knows that in that moment she could faint, scream or drop dead on the spot. Neither of them would notice. She feels a brief flash of excruciating loneliness, then thinks, *my God, you poor bastards*. She imagines that a ghost observing a living person would, if it had the power of conscious thought, think very much the same.

She has been back at her desk for less than half an hour when the phone rings.

'Hi George,' she says, balancing the receiver in the crook of her shoulder and continuing to type.

'How did you know it was me?'

She smiles at her computer screen and decides not to tease him. George and Jerry are in love and Iris feels incredibly superior. She feels in control – for all sorts of reasons.

After their trip to the basement the previous week, Tomlinson went back to being his usual, taciturn self. She was disappointed. She thought they had reached a point of collusion which would be continuous in some way, not closed down as soon as they had marked out their common ground. But it had been useful, all the same. She was able to name what was wrong and once you have named something it is isolated, defined. When you name something – or someone – you take away their power. Iris is learning to be judgmental.

So she feels strong, optimistic – and chooses not to tease the besotted George. She patronises him instead. 'I thought she was really nice,' she says, still looking at her computer screen. 'Very pretty, really, and really outgoing . . . good fun.'

'She's really very clever too,' he says, a little anxiously. 'She's got a very wise head on young shoulders, I mean, well, I think she was probably a bit nervous, meeting you.'

Iris frowns at her screen. 'Why?'

'Well you know, you've got your own business and you know all about the information industry and you're a consultant and so on. You forget that's quite impressive to people, you know.'

'Too right,' she laughs. 'People who have regular jobs always think being self-employed is impressive. We could tell them differently.'

'Anyway,' he continues. 'She liked you too, a lot. She said you were very intelligent . . .' *Cheers Jerry*, Iris thinks sarcastically. 'I suppose she might be a bit jealous too . . .' George continues, 'I've talked about you quite a lot.'

Suddenly, Iris feels overwhelmed with fondness for him. She had assumed that he was ringing to brag but it seems as though he was ringing to reassure. All at once, it occurs to her that maybe George thinks she is his best friend.

'We haven't had a gossip for a while . . .' she suggests.

'That would be nice. Next week some time? You sound a bit more cheerful anyway.'

'I am,' she says. 'And next week would be great. Ring me on Monday.'

As she puts the phone down she wonders why she and George have never got around to exchanging home phone numbers. Somehow, their relationship has always been confined to the province of work. She tries to imagine what he might look like at the weekends but fails. He has always seemed like a man who was born in a suit and tie.

It was only as she returned to her work that she remembered what she had forgotten to ask him: had he dropped by in the last fortnight? Tomlinson had told her that 'the same young man' had asked for her downstairs, again.

She finishes the letter she is working on and prints it out. While she waits for the familiar hum of the laser printer she thinks, *relax, there are no mysteries. Everything is OK now.*

I had frozen in an awkward position. I was leaning forward with one arm outstretched, my weight half on the balls of my feet and half on the other hand, which was splayed against a wooden joist for balance. I knew I couldn't hold it for long. I waited but there was no other sound from downstairs.

If it had only been my ears that had heard the noise then I might have wondered if perhaps I had been mistaken – but my whole body had heard it, and I realised in retrospect that my whole body had been waiting for it. When we transgress, we subconsciously prepare to be caught. I could almost feel its echo in the silence and the long absence of sound that twisted at me as I crouched rigid was filled with intent. Somebody was in the house below me – and they had managed to get as far as the top of the stairs without me hearing a thing. What were they doing now? Did the silence mean that they were frozen too, shivered to stone like me by the sound of the creaking stair? Or were they still on the move, silently? Perhaps, while I was poised on all fours like a small mammal, they were moving inexorably closer. My options were closing down, one by one, with each second that I wasted.

I forced myself to move but with excruciating slowness, like a hundred-year-old woman inching her bones. The sound of my shifting rushed in my ears. I felt sure they would hear the creaking of my muscles.

Iris is in the basement. She is standing in the room full of furniture, where she has narrowed the desks down to a choice of two. One is huge and functional and is easily the most sensible – if there is any way it can be got up to her office. Looking at it, she can't imagine how they even got it down to the basement in the first place. It has a double pedestal with two large drawers on either side and its surface is deep and wide.

Her heart, however, belongs to another. The second desk has a single pedestal, like the one she has already, and its wooden surface is covered with scratches and grazed patches, as though somebody has tried to scrape off some doodles with sandpaper or a scouring brush. It is much older. It would prove an advancement in style but not in function.

She stands back and leans against the wall, surveying the desks and the room. Then she makes her decision.

She turns – but instead of going back to the room of box files and up out of the basement area, she goes the other way, into the smaller room, towards the corridor with the cells.

Gradually, I moved back onto my heels and turned my body in a semi-circle so that I was facing the square hole in the floor of the attic. Around the entrance there was a confusion of light. The bulb above me shone only weakly but a square of strong yellow beamed up from the landing. The aluminium ladder disappeared down into it.

I began to edge towards the entrance. Once there, I felt I would have an advantage. Nobody could climb the ladder without me hearing, and if they did, I would be able to see the top of their head before they saw me.

I had gone less than a foot when the square of yellow was snapped off and I was left washed by the unimpressive glimmer of the faint, elderly bulb above my head. The ladder disappeared and the square leading to the downstairs of the house became a black hole.

They had turned out the landing light.

Iris pauses at the top of the steps. The thick, sprung door is hard behind her back. It feels so solid and real. She cannot believe that anything could come through it. She moves slowly down the steps into the long, low-ceilinged corridor, with its heavy air and strange absence of smell. She can see the mouths of the cells, although she has no intention of going any closer to them in this weak, yellow light. She has not brought a torch. So she sits on the bottom step.

She waits.

I had no idea how long I had been waiting. It could have been ten minutes, maybe it was an hour. Several times, I tried to calculate how much of my remaining life had passed. I remembered my brief and unproductive sojourn as a Girl Guide, when Mrs Walsingham made us all stand up in the Domestic Science block and close our eyes and try to guess how long it was before a minute had passed. When we thought the time was up, we were to sit down and open our eyes.

Afterwards, she told us that none of us had got it right. The only thing to do was to count at an exact, even rate, using the same word to make a space between each number. *One-Mississippi, two-Mississippi, three-Mississippi* . . . Lydia Bennett put her hand up and said her father had told her it was *hippopotamus*.

I had no idea how many seconds had passed while I had been squatting in Peter's attic, but it was long after I ran out of Mississippis and hippopotami.

Iris waits for what feels like a long time. In the meantime, she becomes rather fond of the basement. It has a knowing quality. The only sound is the very distant, constant hum of piping somewhere – which is almost hypnotic. She thinks that it would be a good place to come and meditate once in a while when she wants to get away from her phone. Perhaps she could even bring some work down here.

She stares at her shadow on the nearby wall, too indistinct in the old yellow light to be anything more than a hunched black figure squatting next to one of the cells.

Iris is sitting on the bottom step with her chin in her hands, wearing a smart pleated skirt and matching jacket. Her shadow looks small and huddled down, like an old person in a cape – a portent of what Iris might become.

She smiles at it. She lifts one hand away from her chin and waves it slowly from side to side. The shadow lifts a stunted arm and waves slowly back.

It is at this moment that Iris realises that her shadow is actually at her feet, lying on the floor, attached firmly to its owner, as all shadows should be.

She stares with horror at the black shape on the wall.

Time heals all wounds – and deadens all physical sensation. Squatting there in that attic, I began to doubt. I doubted several things. Firstly, I doubted my ability to accurately assess how many minutes had passed. Then I doubted my sanity – then finally, crucially, I doubted whether or not I had actually heard what I thought I had heard. When I had decided that I had *not* heard the creak of a foot on the stairs, it was relatively easy to move on from there and wonder if perhaps I *had* heard the distinctive pop-pink noise that a light bulb makes when it fuses.

I was going through hoops – but my problem was this. The house was completely silent. How long was I going to squat in the attic?

Slowly, very slowly, Iris rises to her feet. Her real shadow lengthens but the black shape on the wall does not move. Iris keeps her eyes fixed upon it as she backs up the steps. Her heart is pulsing wildly but she is determined not to give in to fear. It might be a trick of the light. Iris will not be tricked any more.

There is only one way to find out.

I unwound my limbs one by one and circled them slowly, creeping towards the hole, as if I was on wheels. Every few seconds I paused, mid-movement, and held my breath, straining to listen.

When I reached the entrance I craned my neck to peer over, down onto the landing.

From this angle, it was not completely dark. A glimmer came from the bulb behind me and the aluminium ladder led down to the pale landing carpeting, like grey Tarmac in the gloom. I could see no-one.

Iris's heel catches on the step behind her. She makes a small, soundless wince. Her right arm is flailing backwards to find the wall. The fingers meet its painted stone surface and scrabble across it, spiderlike. They catch at the metal lightswitch, pass over it in their haste and move swiftly back again.

The switch feels icy cold. Her fingers close around it and push it up. It is stiff. It makes a heavy, resonant click. The room is plunged into thick, irrefutable blackness.

She turns sideways so that her back is up against the wall. She listens.

There was no way I was going slowly down that ladder. I swung myself over the edge in one swift movement and rattled against the steps as I dropped down. There was a clatter of metal as I threw myself back against the landing wall and flattened myself there; freezing, listening.

I could hear nothing. The vague light coming down from the attic was enough to see that there was nobody on the landing but myself. Once I had safely established that, I noticed that my breath was heaving in my chest. I stayed where I was for a moment, feeling the hardness of the wall against my back, my fingers scrabbling over the rough wallpaper for the light switch. I would know as soon as I found it. If the light came on when I flicked it down, then I was not alone.

After a count of three, Iris moves her hand back to the switch, to turn the light on.

The switch isn't there. She sweeps her hand frantically across the wall but there is only a wide expanse of stone. She stops and holds her breath. Please, she thinks, *please*.

If I panic, I will go mad.

She turns and places her palm flat on the wall near to her shoulder. The switch was definitely at shoulder height. All she has to do is move her hand slowly, calmly, across the wall. Her fingers will find the switch.

She begins.

The wall felt smooth before but her fingertips are creeping so slowly that it is now a series of magnified furrows and ridges, slightly warm. It seems to take an age – but eventually her fingers encounter the edge of the square metal plate that surrounds the switch. She exhales. It is only then that she realises she has been holding her breath.

Her fingers slide swiftly across the metal plate – and encounter the soft, fleshy, unmistakable warmth of some-body else's hand.

*

We both screamed.

I don't know which of us actually turned on the light but we ended up bathed in yellow and several feet apart, her at the top of the steps, me at the bottom, crouched down with my fists clenched and pressed into my face, as if the physical discomfort of the position was something to cling onto – the feel of real. I gazed up at her and my expression of huge-eyed shock and recognition was mirrored in her features. She had her back pressed against the door and her knees bent, as if she was trying to shove herself backwards through the solid wood. Both hands were splayed against the door frame, one on either side, holding on for dear life.

Our twin shout echoed up and down the small, low-ceilinged corridor, bouncing around the walls as if it was resonating through history. We had shrieked at the same pitch but the cry grew and shattered. Then the separate elements of it became distorted by the small space in which they were trapped; then welded again as they diminished into a ringing tone which scoured whatever part of the memory retains sound. I will never forget that scream as long as I live.

What remained was not silence. The air was too thick for that. Into the thickness she spoke one word, clearly. 'No.'

I opened my mouth but could not respond. She had seen in an instant who I was – and who she was not. I could only shake my head slowly, looking at her, my gaze hot with pity.

It was then that I remembered the black shape against the wall. I turned. It was still there, although it had shifted a foot to the right. It seemed to be moving up and down slightly, bobbing, making a silent gibber. I knew then that it couldn't speak; not with words, anyway – but it could knock on doors, perhaps, or open them?

'What is that?' Her voice behind me was calm but disgusted.

'I don't know,' I said, 'but it's mischievous. I think . . .' I thought . . . 'I think it is madness.'

I turned back to her. She had sunk down so that she

was squatting on her heels. She stared at me. 'What else is down here?'

I sighed and shrugged, then spread a hand out to indicate that I did not know but that it might be all manner of things.

Her stare became aggressive, making me feel like a magician whose tricks had gone wrong and unleashed a Pandora's box of waifs and demons. I thought she was being a little unfair.

'So what does that make me?' she continued, her voice dense with disappointment, 'like that thing on the wall, just more detailed, a tapestry, whereas that . . .' she pointed at the black shape with an expression of distaste, 'is some obscene graffiti on the door of a toilet.' She looked at me, accusingly. 'I might be more decorative but I'm no more real, am I?'

I could feel my face softening in sympathy. 'You're real to me,' I said, my voice low. 'You're more real than I am.' She looked unconvinced. Involuntarily, my voice became pleading. 'Don't you see? You *are* me.'

For a long moment, we held each other's gaze. Her eyes were just as I had imagined them, clear brown pools large enough to reflect whatever you desired. No wonder men found her irresistible.

Gradually, the focus of her gaze began to melt away from my face and cleave to a space beyond me. Her eyes widened again.

I turned, my body tense, but what I saw filled me with the aching, yearning sensation I had felt when I had first come down here with Tomlinson and he had shone his torch into the black hole of one of the cells.

A woman was gliding towards us. She was small, no more than five feet tall, and young – in her early twenties probably, although her face had the pale, confused openness of a child. Her hair had been cropped short but stuck out all over the place, as if it had been done in a hurry with blunt scissors. She was wearing an ill-fitting brown dress which reached down to the floor. Her feet were wrapped in rags.

There were more rags in her arms, an inanimate bundle of them which looked like several pieces of clothing turned and tied in a swaddling shape. She was clutching the bundle to her chest.

She slid towards us for a few feet, then disappeared.

For a long moment, we were silent. Then I saw that the black shape had gone as well. However deep and specific malevolence may be, it is no match for pity.

I stared at the space where the woman had disappeared. 'Tomlinson's ghost . . .' I said gently. 'The woman . . .'

When I turned back to Bet I saw that she was crying. She had sunk down on the steps and covered the lower half of her face with both hands. Tears welled and flooded. Her slender shoulders dipped and rose. The sound she was making was my own thin, selfish pity made real and substantial by recognition. It came from her guts, deep down inside. It was the kind of crying I could not remember hearing since I was a child.

I had never imagined her crying. (The sobbing over the groceries in the kitchen didn't count.) Bet was not supposed to feel real pain – but she was feeling it now. She was feeling it for her great-gran and for all the generations in between. She was feeling what she could have become had she not escaped the clutches of convention. She was feeling what it might be like to be me.

All at once, I was nauseous with grief; hers – my own.

My eyes began to swim with tears, my chest heaved – and as we both sat there sobbing she began to mist over. Her shape wavered and dissolved. I reached out a hand towards her and blinked frantically but it was too late. She was gone.

I was alone in the empty, empty basement. All my ghosts had disappeared. I was left with the hollow air and thin light and a knowledge of myself so wide and yawning that if I looked too closely I would surely fall in and be swallowed up by it, lost forever to the world.

Given the choice between loneliness and incarceration, which would you choose? At the end of the nineteenth century, they locked a woman up for being what I am now.

I have made a career out of information, as if it is a solid commodity like coffee beans or gold bullion, while knowing that all I am doing is transmitting my own personal form of perception, to which each recipient will bring their own peculiar twist. It is the intellectual equivalent of pass the parcel. Everyone removes a layer optimistically but there always seems to be another layer underneath. Somewhere in there, there may be a kernel of truth but the odds are it will not be you who gets it.

I suffer from something called dissociation. It is a symptom of depression, sometimes psychosis. It is a sort of disconnectedness, the feeling that you are removed from the world around you, that the world around you is not real. I bring to it my own, crypto-egotistical interpretation, of course. For me, it is not the world that is unreal. It is myself.

Psychotics take it to extremes. Serial killers, for instance, manage to serial kill because they reduce their victims to the status of objects; things, not people. The most difficult time must be the first – after that it must be much, much easier. If you have seen the inside of somebody's brain, how can you think of it as anything more than a thing? Perhaps, after that, the problem becomes seeing *anybody* as a person. How do surgeons manage? Is it possible for somebody who has performed a triple heart bypass to ever buy or receive a Valentine's card again? The wonder is not our cruelty but our humanity and humanity lies in our ability to perceive.

The Romans believed in ghosts. Their gods were ghosts, after all, people who had human foibles, likes and dislikes – lost their tempers occasionally and cleaved each other's heads with axes, that sort of thing. The Romans had no concept of the subconscious, or rather, they didn't have the vocabulary to describe it. So the dreams they dreamt or the voices they heard in their heads as they thought about life or the universe or the Emperor's new horse, were all phantoms that seemed disembodied within their skulls, floating around like a shoal of seahorses. In other words, in Roman times, ghosts really did exist.

In the Renaissance, one mind could encompass the whole of human knowledge. All of it could fit inside one person's head.

Now, at the end of the twentieth century, knowledge clings to our brains like detergent foam on the surface of the sea. We know too much and think too clearly. Our thoughts are multi-faceted and bubbled and dissectable – and ineluctably ours. No wonder we are mad.

As the basement's double doors swung shut behind me, I ran up the stairs to the ground floor. At the top I paused. I could go straight up to my office – but I wanted to have a few words with Mr Tomlinson. He had been less than honest with me. I turned right and strode down the corridor.

The door to his room was ajar and I could glimpse him moving around inside. I hesitated, then tapped once, firmly.

As usual, Mr Tomlinson took his time, ambling over to the half-open door with an air that suggested *he* had all day and if *I* didn't then that was *my* problem.

'Mr Tomlinson.' The tone of my voice was intended to make it clear that I was not standing for any nonsense. 'You misled me.'

He looked up at me standing in his doorway, a woman with a chip on her shoulder (a chip the size of Ben Nevis); somebody with a whole wardrobe full of axes to grind; a person who has so many skeletons in her cupboard she can hardly squeeze shut the door. I watched him thinking.

Somebody less perceptive might have thought, what's your problem? Clever, secretive Mr Tomlinson was thinking, you have a great many problems, miss, but I see no reason why any of them should become mine.

'I did not mislead you in any way,' he replied, moving back into his room and continuing his pottering, which as far as I could see involved moving bits of paper from one table to another with the sole purpose of looking far too busy to respond to my accusations. 'I told you what I saw. I never said it was what you were seeing too.'

So he knew what I had come about, without me even explaining. This annoyed me even more. 'You *knew* that my ghost was . . . well, different . . .'

He stopped in the middle of the room, still holding a bit of paper. 'I didn't know, Iris,' he said, and it was the first and last time he ever used my Christian name. 'But when you told me something tapped on your door I knew that there was no way it was the woman I had seen. Whatever it was, she wasn't capable of that, couldn't even think . . .' He was standing in the middle of his little room and suddenly looked small, worn out. 'I don't know what is bothering you,' he said. 'But it's nothing to do with this building.'

The anger, the force of my own certainty, drained out of me and melted into my shoes. My legs felt suddenly weak, as if my bones had liquefied and my torso was being supported by nothing more than two compacted columns of flesh. 'I know,' I said, resignedly, then paused before conceding my next thought. 'I've known all along.'

It took an age to walk back up the stairs to the third floor. I wasn't frightened or angry any more, just tired. Tired beyond belief.

When I reached my office, I pulled the key out of my pocket and pushed it into the lock, then leaned forward with my forehead resting on the door. *Empty*, I thought. I wanted my mind to be empty. It had been so full for so long.

Inside, I tossed the key onto my desk and wandered over to the window but the poignancy and unorginality of the view was more than I could bear. I sank into my chair and leaned back. I closed my eyes.

'Bet,' I said softly.

There was a momentary pause, then I felt her behind me. I looked around. She was leaning back against the wall. In the white light of the office I could see her more clearly than I had been able to down in the basement. She was just as I had imagined her: tall, long-limbed, in a pose that suggested the wall had been constructed specifically for her to lean against.

She gave a half-smile. 'What do you think?' she said.

'I think it's time to let go,' I replied sadly.

She didn't respond.

'But if I let go of you, then I let go of . . . everything, all of it, the grief . . .'

'The pain . . .'

I turned away from her. 'You wouldn't think that would be difficult to let go of would you?' I said to the wall.

'That's the most difficult thing of all,' she said. 'That's when you really are at sea . . .'

I didn't speak for a long time. I couldn't bring myself to look at her again but I could see her out of the corner of my eye, a blurry shape against the wall, like something you might glimpse in passing which would turn – when you blinked – into a shadow.

'Come on . . .' she said eventually, coaxing, understanding. 'Time to finish me off.'

10

*B*et has frozen in an awkward position. She is leaning forward with one arm outstretched, her weight half on the balls of her feet and half on the other hand, which is splayed against a wooden joist for balance. She knows she can't hold it for long. She waits but there is no other noise from downstairs.

It is as if her whole body has heard the creak on the stairs – and she realises now that her whole body had been waiting for it. She can feel the echo of the noise through the silence and the absence of sound that twists her as she crouches rigid is filled with intent. Somebody is in the house below her – and they have managed to get as far as the top of the stairs without her hearing a thing. What are they doing? Does the silence mean that they too are frozen, shivered to stone like her by the creaking of the stair? Or are they still on the move, silently? Perhaps, while she is poised on all fours like a small mammal, they are moving inexorably closer. Her options are closing down, one by one, with each second that she wastes.

She forces herself to move but with excruciating slowness, like a hundred-year-old woman inching her bones. The sound of her shifting rushes in her ears. She feels sure they will hear the creaking of her muscles.

Gradually, she moves back onto her heels and turns her body in a semi-circle so that she is facing the square hole in the floor of the attic. Around the entrance there is a confusion of light. The bulb above her shines only weakly but a square of strong yellow beams up from the landing. The aluminium ladder disappears down into it.

She begins to edge towards the entrance. Once there, she feels she will have an advantage. Nobody can climb the ladder without her hearing and if they do, she will be able to see the top of their head before they see her.

She has nearly reached the square hole when she hears something else: the creak of metal. She freezes. Her ears try to re-register the noise, to work out whether somebody has just touched the aluminium ladder or is trying to climb it. The sound was insubstantial, accidental – and somehow, the lightness of it gives Bet courage. She pokes her head over the hole and looks down.

Iris makes a gurgled scream and falls back off the ladder.

Bet is so surprised that she jumps back from the hole, slips on the wooden joist and puts a foot straight through a thin layer of plaster into the hall below. She is still cursing and swearing when Iris calls up from the hall. 'God . . . god, what's happened? Are you OK?'

'My foot . . .' Bet responds furiously. 'Bloody hell Iris,

what the hell are you doing creeping around. Why didn't you ring the bloody bell?'

Iris climbs the aluminium ladder far enough for her head and shoulders to appear through the hole. Bet sits back on the joist and examines her leg. Her jeans have protected her, although they are scraped and flecked with plaster. She rubs at her calf through the tough denim. It feels as though she has pulled a muscle, probably as she yanked her leg back.

She turns to Iris and crawls towards the hole. 'Let me out of here,' she mutters, 'you gave me the fright of my life. Go and put the kettle on.'

Iris backs down the aluminium ladder but once at the bottom she does not go down to the kitchen as ordered. She waits.

'Are you all right?' she asks Bet as she descends.

'No thanks to you . . .' Bet says, pausing at the bottom of the ladder to brush herself down. She looks at Iris, who has no make-up on and is dressed in an old grey cardigan and black leggings. Her long fair hair needs washing and is pulled back in a band.

'I've still got my key,' Iris says, sheepishly. 'I told Peter I'd thrown it away. I didn't think he'd believe me. I thought the locks would have been changed. I tried it just to see and when it opened I thought that now was my chance. I had a look downstairs but I couldn't find anything. I'm sorry if I frightened you.'

'You're a twit,' says Bet, not unkindly. 'I might have hit you with something.'

Iris looks up into the attic. Bet looks with her and thinks, *dark*. Funny how dark it looks up there from down here. And when you get up there it is just unclear, that's all.

'I suppose . . .' Iris says.

'Yes,' says Bet, 'I found out all about Peter's little business.'

'Did you . . . ?'

'No. Nothing. What is it, a video?'

Iris nods miserably.

Bet sighs. 'Come on. Let's go downstairs. I want a drink. You can fill me in with the details.' She turns to go but Iris does not move. So Bet turns back and says, 'Afterwards, you can go up there and take away whatever you want, I promise. I don't want anything to do with it.'

Iris sits curled up on the sofa in the sitting-room. It is a large sofa, covered with plain, taut grey linen. She is tucked into one corner of it with her legs folded underneath her body. She looks small.

She is nursing the large whisky which Bet has poured. Bet has a similar one – only her glass was more full to start off with but is already more empty. She is sitting cross-legged on the floor.

Iris is talking but she is not looking at Bet. Her gaze has settled hypnotically upon a patch of space suspended between them. Her words skim the top of her glass and dissolve into the air, as if she wants to pretend they do not belong to her after they have left her mouth.

'I met him at a party. We were in bed within hours. I'd

never done that before. It seemed so straightforward, so natural.' Her mouth twisted into a tiny smile. It was a smile full of pain. 'Funny thing was, he seemed to want me so badly at the time, he sort of seduced me I suppose. But later, a couple of months later when things were going wrong, he told me he would have preferred it if I had said no.' She shakes her head. 'I couldn't understand that. They ask you to have sex with them but they don't want to? Or they want to but they want you *not* to want to? But I thought they wanted to be wanted. I don't understand . . .' Her voice falters and her gaze drifts. Then she comes round.

'It was very, well, intense is the word I suppose. We spent the whole day in bed once, one weekend. Do you know I'd never done that before? It was a Sunday and we slept in late and then had breakfast and then dozed again and it was winter and somehow before we knew it, it was dark. It was as if it had never got light, as if we had stopped that day from happening, like when you are ill and time has stopped, you've made the whole world suspended – sort of sick, sick but beautiful. He was so determined about me. Much more so than anyone else I had been out with. And possessive. Those first few weeks, it was quite something . . .'

Her voice has softened as she has been speaking, as if the memory is so clear that the flavour of it has temporarily overwhelmed her other senses. Then, her face darkens. 'He said he wanted to take the pictures because I was so beautiful. But I knew, if I'm honest. I knew there was something funny about it. He was so efficient, clinical. I think I must have known it was something he had done before. The video . . .' She pauses. Her gaze becomes milky. 'I was drunk at the time.'

'So you weren't the first,' says Bet.

Iris gives a bitterly ironic laugh. 'I doubt it very much. No, he was far too practised for that.'

'The police?'

Iris throws Bet a scornful look. 'It isn't illegal you know. It isn't even illegal to sell them, not if you keep within the guidelines.'

'Where did they go?'

'Through Europe I think, the laws are lighter. Sophie and Alex handled that side of it. Quite profitable I think, although they do other things as well.'

Bet moves backwards and waves an arm in a sudden gesture of frustration. 'Why didn't you *do* something?'

Iris stays very still, peering over her glass of whisky. Then she looks down into it as if she has only just remembered it is there. 'Peter gave me a choice. Well, he made it sound like a joke but I got the message. If I didn't make a fuss, the stuff went abroad. If I did, then it went out to the home market. And . . .' She takes a gulp of her drink, swills it once around her mouth and then tosses her head back, as if she is swallowing a pill. 'And by then I was pregnant.'

Bet remembers the infant. 'Where's your son?' she asks.

'With a neighbour,' Iris replies.

Bet pauses. 'Is he Peter's?' she asks.

Iris is unmovable. She might have turned into a block

of wood. When her voice comes, it is thick with incomprehension. 'I don't know. I was married at the time.'

My God, what a mess, Bet thinks sadly. What a fearful, terrible mess some people make of their lives. Sophie had been right about Iris, in some ways. She was a victim. She had entered into an affair with Peter against her better judgment and then she had let it continue when she must have known she was heading for disaster. Her behaviour was not stupid: it was something more subtle and specific, a combination of ignorance and weakness and narcissism – the talent all victims share. But Sophie was wrong in other ways. Just because Iris had been a victim, did not mean that Peter was unaccountable for his actions.

'Come on . . .' Bet slaps both hands down on her knees then rises. Iris looks up, a little alarmed.

'Where?' she asks.

'We have work to do,' Bet says briskly, taking the glass from Iris's hand. 'Sophie and Alex are due round here tomorrow and we've got to head them off at the pass.' She takes both their glasses through to the kitchen, talking over her shoulder as she goes. 'There are some big cardboard boxes in the pantry here, but it's going to take several trips all the same. You'd better ring that neighbour and explain you're going to be late back. Very late.'

It takes hours.

Bet sends Iris up into the attic first, alone, to look for what she wants. While she is up there, she goes round the house and collects as many plastic bags as she can find. She also checks the Thompson Local Directory and discovers several words that rhyme with *waste*. One company has a taste for it. Another advises her to make haste. The second has a twenty-four-hour hotline so she makes a call. They are very understanding when she explains that she doesn't want anything collecting, just some information about where to take it.

As she puts the phone down, she hears Iris climbing down from the attic, rattling the aluminium ladder. She goes upstairs and finds her leaning against the landing wall, in tears. She stops and stands in front of her, wondering what to say.

Iris has both hands splayed meaninglessly across her face. She is sobbing her stupidity into the hands. 'It could be any of them,' she gulps. 'I've no idea what all that stuff is. I thought I'd recognise it. He showed it to me . . .'

'Oh Iris . . .' Bet sighs her irritation, but indulgently. 'We can't go through them all, even if we had time it would hardly make edifying viewing. You're going to have to trust me.'

Iris continues as if Bet hasn't spoken. 'Suppose there are copies with Alex and Sophie? And anyway it probably went out anyway. There could be hundreds of copies floating around, anywhere.'

Bet leans forward and takes hold of Iris's elbows, pulling at her arms gently so that she has to remove her hands from her face. 'Listen to me,' she says firmly into Iris's moist, puffy face. 'There is nothing we can do about anything outside this house. You did something stupid

201

and you're going to have to live with it, but we can get rid of everything here, and we can make sure you don't get bothered by Alex and Sophie. If you don't want to take anything up there away then we have to get rid of it, the lot of it. It's going to take ages.'

It does.

Afterwards, Iris pours them two more whiskys, both large this time, while Bet sits at Peter's shiny dining table and writes a note which she will have delivered to Sophie and Alex the following morning.

Dear Sophie and Alex

Thank you for your kind offer of help but I have done my own search of Peter's house and found what I think you were after. I take it that when you said bearer shares you actually meant barer.

I have thrown nearly everything away. Iris has helped me. The equipment, the lists and the videos have all gone to the dump where, by the time you read this, they will have been incinerated.

I have kept some photos and some computer diskettes and they are lodged with a solicitor. They will stay there indefinitely, untouched, unless anything unexpected happens to me.

Do not contact me, or Iris, ever again, by any means whatsoever.

Yours,

Bet.

P.S. Sophie. Have you thought of waxing your arm-pits? I know that shaving is quicker and more convenient but there was a bit of stubble showing.

*

Maybe even pornographers are capable of love, Bet thinks as she folds Peter's dressing-gown. She pauses.

It is some weeks later. She is in the bedroom, standing by the bed, which is now stripped down to its king-size mattress. Sitting on the bare mattress is an open suitcase which contains a few remaining things of her own and one or two items of Peter's which she has decided she wants: a couple of nice cotton shirts, the volcano table mat – just for a laugh. Beside her, on the floor, squats a black plastic bag full of Peter's suits, waiting to be tied up and taken down to Help the Aged.

She was about to add the dressing-gown to the suits but has a second thought and drops it into her case.

It is silk but that is not why she is taking it. She wants it because it reminds her of the pleasant parts of her grief, her early moments alone in Peter's house, the mornings when she rose late, bewildered, knowing that there was a great deal to discover. It was a period of her life that seems so sad and strange and distant, it has taken on an odd sort of glamour and poignancy. She nursed the loss of him as she might have nursed a child.

Now, there is no feeling left; but even so she understands,

now, why some people cannot let go of grief. She understands how it is possible to love a shadow.

She moved back to her own flat the day after she and Iris cleaned out the attic but has been coming back intermittently to pick things up. Most of Peter's personal detritus has gone into the dustbin. Anything useful went to the charity shops. The smaller pieces of furniture are piled in the sitting-room. The larger pieces are still in place, waiting for the auctioneer's men to come and tag them and remove them. The carpets and curtains have been left where they are because the estate agent said the house would go more quickly if it wasn't stripped completely bare. She has told him she will take the first offer. Somebody is going to get a bargain.

She closes the suitcase. Then she turns and ties the top of the black plastic bag. Both bag and case are half-empty, so she carries them downstairs at the same time, one in each hand.

She has grown rather fond of the Mini. It is orange, rusting, and makes an unbelievable grinding noise when she goes round a corner – but she thinks she will hang onto it. It feels like hers. She swings the case onto the passenger seat and tosses the bag into the back. Then she turns back to the house. Perhaps she should have one last look round.

She steps inside the front door, and pauses. The hallway with its cold parquet flooring is empty and bare. The small table and phone are gone and the absence of these two simple items seems to have created vast amounts of space. Already, the hall has attained the dusty, deadened aspect that all places acquire when they have been empty for some time.

She turns resolutely and goes back out. *Last looks round* are for wimps. Bet is not a wimp.

She slams the front door behind her and drops the keys through the letter box, for the estate agent to pick up when he lets himself in with his own set, later that afternoon. He is showing a young couple round.

She stands in the drive, looking up at the house with her arms folded, and allows herself a brief, self-indulgent moment of reflection. He is dead, she thinks.

Brave and beautiful, promiscuous and proud, Bet has fulfilled both her dream and her function. She has laid a ghost.

11

*F*antasies are cosy things, more than cosy they are wild, consoling, warm – and infinite. Above all, they are so private that you can behave as outrageously as you please and there is not the remotest chance that you will ever be humiliated.

When I parade in front of my mirror, I often fantasise that I am so extraordinarily beautiful that somebody (intelligent, witty, and not bad-looking themselves) is staring at me in amazement, shaking their head in awe.

Sane people have no idea what they're missing.

My gaze came back into focus. The office felt icily still. I rose and returned to the window, then grasped the bottom sash and lifted it an inch or two, to let the coldness out. A fresh spring breeze blew briskly, snappily in. There were the sudden sounds of distant traffic and the faint roar of an invisible passing plane.

The phone rang.

It was Mr James of James Chemical & Hygiene Co Ltd, who wanted to let me know that he had read the marketing plan and thought it was fine work, as usual. There were just a few points that he wanted to correct. I found myself saying, 'Yes of course Mr James, your input is always so constructive.' I actually said that, without the merest hint of sarcasm or self-irony.

While I was talking to him, I reached out for my copy of the plan, which had been sitting in my *pending* tray for weeks, awaiting this call. I lifted a red pen from the plastic tray of biros to the right of my computer. I managed to annotate the plan, discuss it with him, and arrange a time for me to visit them in Middlesex without thinking about any of it at all. I was dissociated from Mr James and his chemical company. I was not the Iris that he thought he was talking to. I was no more real than a blow-up doll with her mouth poised in a receptive, uncritical O.

The phone's reciever had only just hit the cradle when it rang again. My hand performed a swift U-turn. 'Iris Farrow?'

There was a momentary pause, then Tomlinson's voice said, 'Gentleman downstairs to see you.'

An alarm bell rang somewhere in my subconcious, a premonition. 'Who?' I asked shortly.

'Young man I mentioned before,' Tomlinson replied, 'he's out front.'

'I'll come down,' I said, not that Tomlinson would be expecting me to do anything else.

I picked up my handbag and slammed the office door shut behind me. Just past the swing doors I hesitated, then turned swiftly into the ladies'. I peered at myself in the grimy, dappled mirror, side-lit by the muddled light from a nearby frosted pane of glass. I looked pale. I always did look pale in that mirror. I leant forward and pulled a face which elongated my upper lip and widened my eyes. Then I drew a finger underneath each row of lower lashes, clearing the two slight smudges of make-up which had gathered there.

I walked swiftly down the corridor. The lift was waiting for me, doors open.

Tomlinson was standing in the doorway of his little room, chewing something. He gestured towards the entrance. 'He's out there. Said he wanted to wait outside.' Then he turned and went back into his room.

It could have been anyone waiting for me on the steps. It could have been a delivery boy or a photocopier engineer. It could have been George, wanting to ask whether he could come up and use my terminal for half an hour because he was downloading sixty pages of graphics on his and needed to send a quick e-mail.

But it wasn't. It was Peter.

He looked both different and exactly the same. He looked different because when you haven't seen somebody for several months, the image of their features becomes static in the mind's eye. You forget how much movement can change a face. He looked exactly the same because when you see that face again the memory of the way it moves comes rushing back. You recall things you were not aware of having forgotten.

I remembered that although Peter was often awkward, bodily, his gaze was always very sure. When he looked at you, he seemed on the point of asking a question.

He was wearing a coat I had not seen before, a dark brown suede jacket. He was standing on the bottom step with his toes over the edge, arms folded, rocking slightly as if he was contemplating jumping off. He turned quickly when he heard my approach. His face was slightly reddened by the cold. He was wearing his glasses. His hair was shorter than I remembered and I was suddenly aware that my hair would be shorter too – I had had it cut since we last saw each other. I pushed a hand through my dark, floppy fringe, then realised that the gesture was nervous and lowered the hand quickly. I flicked a smile.

He looked at me and said, 'I know you're probably really busy. I was just passing.' Then he gave a broad grin, the sort of grin you return as a reflex action. He lifted both his arms briefly then dropped them to his side. 'Bit of a surprise eh? Sorry. Take a break for a few minutes. I haven't got any real reason or anything. I just thought it would be nice. We could have a drink later if you like or tea now. Nothing in particular.'

I felt briefly offended that he felt obliged to emphasise that this was nothing more than a casual, dropping-by little chat. Did he think that I might be hoping he would fall on one knee and propose? I considered pretending that I was too busy but I knew I couldn't do it convincingly. He had caught me off-guard. And anyway, if I sent him away, he would think that I was still so upset that I couldn't cope with talking to him. He would walk away thinking, *poor Iris, she still finds it difficult*. Pride got the better of me – and anyway, I was curious.

'Tea,' I said, gesturing. 'Tea and cake or something. There's a place up the road.'

We began to walk.

The air was confusing. It was the end of March. Soon, the clocks would go back – or was it forward? I could never remember which but I could remember that March was the month when an hour was lost, a whole hour of time that would somehow slip into a fold in existence, like a penny falling down the back of a sofa, its currency still extant but unavailable. When I was little, I used to worry about it.

It was just over five months since we had split up amidst a great deal of wailing and acrimony – but it was a whole year since I had realised that Peter didn't love me. Almost exactly a year – I knew because of that lost hour.

This was the month when the weather was a constant panorama, an ever-changing vista of breeze-driven cloud and rain punctuated by air raids of sudden sunshine. In the time it took to walk to the post-box you could be reaching for your umbrella or sunglasses or both. Neurotics like me never knew what to expect.

I had come out without my coat so I wore my forearms crossed over my chest.

'Is your heater working these days?' said Peter suddenly, as we strode along.

I threw a glance his way.

'You know, your heater, you always had problems with it I remember.'

I recalled a whole, insignificant conversation we had once had, back in the days when we had insignificant conversations. I had complained about how difficult it was to get my office warm enough without it becoming stuffy to work. When the convector heater was turned on, it was too hot. When it was turned off the room was freezing. During the process of the heater going on or off, however, there would be a brief, ambient period when the temperature was just right. I was forever leaping up from my desk to switch the damn thing on or off. My working day was a succession of sweats and shivers.

This had been a noteworthy part of my life when I first moved into the office, while Peter and I were still going out with each other. Now it was just one of a hundred tiny details which formed the backdrop of my existence. It seemed an odd thing for Peter to have remembered.

'Like the weather in March,' I said. 'The way it changes all the time.'

The apparent non sequitur didn't seem to bother him. He didn't comment.

All at once I realised that he didn't know what to say to me. A thought crashed about my head. He is more nervous than I am. He is more *bothered* than me.

We turned the corner.

'You're going to Philip's this weekend,' he stated lightly

211

as we settled in our seats and he unloaded our tray of tea, coffee and cake.

I had selected something huge and sticky made of chocolate, with nuts clinging to its sludgy dark-brown surface. I didn't particularly want it but I needed something to play with in case the conversation became difficult. I also had a pot of Earl Grey with lemon slices on a saucer.

Peter had a black filter coffee.

'How do you know?' I asked.

'I was talking to Alex, he'd seen Susan in the pub.'

I felt annoyed with all of them for gossiping about me – and pleased. 'It's Sammy's birthday tea, family get-together. Susan rang me up and gave me the three line whip on Philip's behalf.'

'I saw Marianne at the market a couple of weeks ago,' Peter said. Marianne was Philip's wife, my sister-in-law, a placid woman who baked excellent cakes. I wondered where all this was leading.

'I was with someone actually,' Peter said as he took a sip of his coffee – and suddenly I knew what was coming. There was time for me to absorb the information before it arrived. There was even time for me to absorb the shock of it – and to come out the other side. 'Nobody you know, someone I've known for a while. She's living with me at the moment. Actually, we're thinking about getting married.'

I was trapped. There was no way I could respond which he could not interpret as me being upset. Trying to affect nonchalance was potentially the most humiliating of all options, so I simply smiled icily and said, 'Congratulations.'

'I thought maybe I should tell you, in person,' he said, although at this point he would not meet my gaze. 'I thought there was bound to be talk at Philip's.' *Yeah, that's right, we'll have nothing better to do than talk about you.* 'I hope you don't ... well. Maybe we could all meet up some time.' *I would rather spend an evening chewing dead rats and light bulbs.* 'We'll probably take the plunge in the summer some time. We haven't quite made up our minds.'

'Alex and Sophie must be overjoyed,' I said, knowing that the true depth of sarcasm in my voice would be lost on him.

'I saw Alex yesterday,' Peter said, frowning. 'You never liked him much did you?'

There was no reason for me to pretend otherwise, now. 'Alex always struck me as the sort of man who reads dirty magazines on the side.'

Peter leapt predictably to his defence. 'All men read dirty magazines on the side,' he said dismissively, reminding me of how offhand he had always been whenever I said anything remotely critical about any man of our acquaintance.

'You mean all the men you know do,' I replied coolly.

He raised his eyebrows and looked at me.

We had moved into a sensitive topic. I didn't want to have a fight so I added quickly, 'How's Sophie?'

Peter pulled a face. 'They're going through a bad patch, actually. It's all a bit tricky at the moment. The boat business isn't very good.'

I prevented myself from smirking. The thought of Alex and Sophie having economic problems was immensely gratifying. 'What about the helicopter business?'

At this, Peter brightened. We were off the subject of his impending marriage and his friends and onto what he loved best.

He chatted about the funding problems at the hospital and how glad the pilots were that they were employees of the private air ambulance sponsor and not the NHS. Then he launched into a lengthy anecdote about a trick he had played on Mike, when they had flown down to Surrey, to pick up some equipment from a field. It had been raining and the worms had all come to the surface when they felt the helicopter's vibrations. While Mike had been loading up the pack, Peter had put worms in his headphones. He knew it was a stupid thing to do, of course. He wouldn't have done it if they'd had a patient in the back. But it had been ever so funny.

I sat picking at my cake with a teaspoon thinking, I used to listen to this several times a week. I was as glad as him, however, to have got off the subject of marriage – and even more so – Alex and Sophie. Why was it, I wondered as Peter chuntered on, that their small betrayal rankled so much more than Peter's large one?

They had made my humiliation seem public. They had been the mirror in which Peter and I had been shown for

what we were – a careless, lying man and a woman too
weak to do anything about it. Inwardly, I shuddered.

We parted on the stone steps of my office building. We
murmured about getting together some time. I did a lot
of shrugging. Peter had an uncharacteristic fit of gallantry
and said how well I was looking and how nice it would
be to see me properly some time.

   We said our goodbyes and I turned quickly up the steps
so that he would be obliged, if only momentarily, to watch
me climb up and away from him.

   There is no such thing as laying a ghost, I thought as I
pushed through the doors. It's never as tidy as that. They
will always pop up again just when you thought you had
seen the back of them.

   I knew that Peter would be walking away feeling pleased
with himself, thinking that it had been the right thing to
do, dropping by, telling me about his marriage personally
– thinking, perhaps, that as I had clearly forgiven him for
dumping me so unceremoniously then he probably wasn't
such a bad bloke after all. I knew that according to Peter's
own twisted, immutable logic, he would have won some
small victory that afternoon.

   I didn't care.

'I saw Peter yesterday,' I said and my therapist stared at
me, waiting. When it was clear that I would not proceed
without a signal from her, she said, 'And how did you
feel about that?'

'Dead,' I said. I waited for a few moments, to keep her company. 'Dead in the good sense of the word, though. Dead in all the right places. He's getting married. Not sure whether it's the woman he dumped me for or someone else. He said I didn't know her. I didn't like to ask for further details. He didn't volunteer so I suppose that means it's her. I was a bit taken aback of course, although I had been expecting it somehow. Afterwards I felt as though I had conjured him, at that particular moment. It seemed so appropriate. That was all it seemed – appropriate for me, for my scheme of things. For him, emotionally I mean, I felt nothing. Dead in the heart – and from the waist down thank God. It's gone. I think, finally, it's gone.'

It was only towards the end of our session that she said, 'I do think we should talk a bit about why you haven't come here lately.'

It was the first time I had been for six weeks. The last time, I had dressed up and fooled around – teased, flirted, evaded. She had been quite irritable. I had left before the end of the session.

I began to talk about how bad things had been. I began to talk about the blackouts, the paranoia – the length of the periods of dissociation, whole afternoons in my office fantasising, lost. I told her that I had been to see a new GP to get myself checked out, hoping, as usual, that what was wrong was something simple and physical. I was embarrassed to admit that. I had been through so many periods of clinical depression that denial was really something I should have worked through.

216

She listened to me with infinite care, as always, allowing herself the very slightest of smiles when I told her that I had gone to a new GP because the old one only asked me how my therapy was going and never did so much as take my blood pressure.

I didn't mention Bet. I may do, one day, but for the time being Bet is mine. To share her with someone else would be to diminish her. It would make her into something explicable, like a throat virus. I am not ready for that, not yet.

Instead, I talked about the pain. I had a vocabulary for that. I talked about the feeling I had when I woke each morning, as if I had spent the night swimming in cold porridge – the horror of it, the involuntary sickening at the thought that I am conscious again.

She tipped her head to one side slightly. 'In other words,' she said carefully, 'you have stayed away when you have needed me most.'

I could say nothing in response. I was incapable of movement, so she supplied the nod.

That Sunday, I arrived at Philip's to find the house in uproar and Peter's forthcoming marriage – or, for that matter, my existence – to be matters remote to the assembled throng. Sammy, the birthday boy, was two years old, but the herd of children stampeding up and down the stairs came in a wide variety of shapes and sizes. As I stepped inside the open front door, a tiny whirly thing in a Superman costume careered head first into my knees, spun once, then hit the floor. I paused and looked down, wondering if it had hurt itself, but it leapt to its feet, punched the air with its fist, then flattened itself against the hallway mirror, where it stuck like a fly.

Marianne came down the hallway. 'Hi Iris,' she said, peeling the child off the mirror and shoving it gently in the direction of the sitting-room. 'Glad you're here. They outnumber us by about ten to one at the moment. The four-year-olds have formed a group and are about to march on the town hall.' I used to think that Marianne was a dull old stick but since having her third child she seems to have acquired a sense of humour. Perhaps by that stage it is a prerequisite.

I was touched that she seemed to think I was going to be some use amongst the chaos but I knew better. My function would be restricted to laying out paper cups and plates and nodding at other adults over the heads of their offspring. Sammy was my favourite but I knew I wouldn't get near him.

I walked into the sitting-room where the table had been extended and the birthday tea was nearly ready for the impending hurricane. Two other mums were helping Marianne put the finishing touches to the piles of sandwiches, crisps and cakes. They smiled hello and I joined them. I was being ushered into a seat at the end of the table when a voice from the doorway called, 'Aunty *Iris!*'

Standing in the doorway was Mina, my six-year-old niece. 'Hello Mina,' I said, and held out my arms for her to come and climb on my lap, which she occasionally consented to do. This time she shook her head solemnly and looked over at a pale child standing next to her whose hand she was clutching for dear life.

'Lydia,' said one of the other mums, a thin, gingery-haired woman whose name I couldn't recall. 'She's mine. She and Mina are best friends at the moment. They're obsessed with each other. They have to hold hands all the time, even when they're going through doorways.' Mina and Lydia squeezed themselves into the sitting-room shoulder-to-shoulder, like a miniature set of Tweedle Dum and Tweedle Dee. Then they made their way to the table where they clambered awkwardly onto adjoining chairs and sat, still clutching hands, glancing first at the heavily laden table, then at each other, with expressions of awe.

Eventually, Marianne succeeded in rounding up the rest of them and we were all assembled. At this point my brother Philip deigned to put in an appearance. He appeared at the doorway with his beard and open-necked shirt, holding his camcorder, a tiny thing that fitted snugly in the palm of one hand and almost as securely against Philip's right eye.

The camcorder came out on all family occasions, sacred or profane, and Philip spent much of his time viewing the world through its small, refracting lens. He now stood surveying the table with it, his body tense with concentration. As its one-eyed stare reached me he raised the flat of his hand in greeting. As he pointed it at each of the children in turn, they became solemn and still, only breaking into smiles when it had safely passed.

The only child who was not seated was Marianne and Philip's middle one, four-year-old Joe. He had been standing at one corner of the table, quietly, ever since he had entered the room. Directly in front of him was a plateful of small cakes decorated with lurid-coloured icing. He was staring at the plate with round eyes and a steady, purposeful gaze, waiting for the off, clearly intent on bypassing the sandwiches and sausage rolls and going straight for the main business, which was to cram as much sugar as would fit into his small stomach.

'Come on everybody,' Marianne hollered, waving a hand.

We began to eat. I watched Joe as he ploughed gallantly through the plate of cakes in front of him. The other children were all putting food on their side plates but Joe had decided to cut out the middle man. He did pretty well. In ten minutes, over half the plate had gone. No-one spoke to him throughout the meal, which was just as well. His cheeks were bulging and he was quite green. But he had the vacant, determined gaze of the man who had set himself a serious and vital task and was resolved to plough on to the bitter-sweet end.

I left him to it and turned my attention to young Samuel, the ostensible star of the show, seated in his high chair next to his mother at the far end of the table. I waved at him, smiling in that idiotic, aunty-ish sort of way and he lifted a fat hand and waved back. Small pieces of cake flew from his fingers. He had taken a somewhat inventive approach to his birthday tea. Instead of eating it, he had decided to wear it.

Later, we all broke from the table and the children returned to the serious task of wrecking the house. Philip had threatened to organise games but for the time being occupied himself by pursuing fleeing youngsters with his camcorder while the women cleared up the chaos.

Marianne insisted that I sat down in an adjacent armchair and had a rest, although I had done nothing much. We talked lightly about my other brother and his family who had gone down to Bournemouth to spend the weekend with our parents. The official line was that it was a shame that they couldn't all be there, although I sensed relief in Marianne's voice. The two wives didn't get on.

So I settled in my chair, like the idle career girl that they all supposed me to be, and watched my sister-in-law as she simultaneously tidied up, brought tea through for all the adults and looked after twenty children. I thought how well she fitted into my family, how much better than myself.

As I observed the happy, muddled group around me I could feel myself detaching, as if I was having one of those out-of-body experiences that people have when they die on the operating table, as if I was floating above these cheerful, disorganised folk and looking down from a position of lofty if solitary superiority.

A two-year-old called Gemma paddled past me. She was lying on her stomach and moving herself forward by flailing her arms and legs against the carpet, like a turtle. Her face wore an expression of intense concentration, as well it might. She was progressing a centimetre at a time and having to jut her chin forward to prevent it scraping on the floor. Marianne had placed a cup of tea beside my chair. I lifted it to safety and took a sip, then scratched my leg, feeling remote and self-absorbed.

However big or small they are, relations are Lilliputians, each with a tiny cord which binds you to the earth. If you could take them on one at a time, you could snap yourself free in a second – but it is a lot more complex than that. They make up more than the sum of their parts. They each form a strand of the huge, binding web of love that tethers you to your place in the world.

It's messy, that's all. It is messy being loved.

Later, I went to see Susan. I drove through the Sunday streets in the battered orange Mini that Peter used to laugh at. The teasing had an edge, I always thought. Peter wouldn't have been seen dead driving a car like mine. I didn't mind him mocking it because of its deficiencies as a car – what I minded was the feeling that he was mocking it because it was mine. The car I owned was a symptom of my not being good enough.

The streets seemed unbelievably quiet. I drove slowly, enjoying my autonomy.

Maybe one day I would be prepared to do all that, what Philip and Marianne had done. Perhaps there would come a time when I would want to crash land my life, to let it explode with the clamour and colour of children. Maybe one day I would revel in it. But not now, not yet. Not for a long time yet.

Susan had been in for only ten minutes. Her house was similar to my flat, style-wise, but tidier. Three years ago, she had bought a tiny terrace with some money her grandparents had left her and spent another small fortune knocking down walls and landscaping a square of grass out the back. She rewired the place herself.

She had just returned from visiting her father in the nursing home and felt the same as me: knackered, happy to be free, in need of a drink. Gin and tonic, she declared, with a slice of lime. She had bought the lime specially the previous day.

I perched on a kitchen stool while she eased ice cubes out of their plastic container, watching her and thinking happily, *this is my friend*. This is my life.

There was a glimmer of sun so it was almost warm outside. We pushed back the patio doors and stepped out onto the landscaped patch of grass and Susan chatted idly about underpinning. Then we did a tour of her tiny garden, nursing our drinks, and I thought that wandering and talking like this to a friend is surely one of the most romantic things that anyone could do.

There is one more part of the story to be told.

If friends can be romantic, then they can also be treacherous. Let us not get misty-eyed about platonic relationships. We are all capable of sabotage.

Perhaps that is misleading. Alex and Sophie were always more Peter's friends than mine. There was no reason for me to expect any particular loyalty from them. It was Peter's fault, really. He gave them a big build-up, referring to them airily as his *best* friends, whatever that means, making it clear that acceptance from them was an important step on the road into his life. We went out together as a foursome several times, that's all, and away for the weekend once. I always felt pathetically grateful when it went well.

It was on one of those dates that I realised – no, discovered – that Peter was promiscuous.

Sophie was wearing a blue dress. She glowed that evening. She was the kind of woman other women do not envy but who makes them feel a little bewildered; about being a woman, about what men want. The soft curls, the snubbed nose, the sprinkling of freckles – there was plumpness in her arms and a babyish whine in her voice that, to me, sounded cultivated. 'Sophie's great,' Peter said, the first time we discussed them. 'She's very sweet.'

We were in booths in an American-style rib-and-burger restaurant. The men were having huge racks of ribs – great, glistening lumps of meat and bone – but then Peter and Alex were meaty kinds of men.

I don't object to meat but I like it well disguised, so I had opted for lasagne. Sophie was having a prawn salad.

The boys were in a good mood, boisterous, ordering beer to start off with, then far too much wine and talking loudly over the heavy, transatlantic guitar that thumped

224

from nearby speakers. Peter seemed more affectionate and attentive than usual, pressing his thigh up against mine underneath the table and reaching out a hand to ruffle the hair on the back of my head. Alex leant sideways towards Sophie and dropped a piece of slimy, marinated meat down her cleavage. She squealed in horror and we all laughed fit to bust.

I suppose that is what should have warned me. There was a fragile quality to our laughter, a sense of strain. We were all trying just that little bit too hard to have a good time.

I realised all this in retrospect but at the time I was too awash with relief for it to register. Things had not been going well between Peter and myself. He had been irritable. I had been clingy. In my heart of hearts, I knew I was losing him.

It was because of the music, and because we were sitting in a booth. If we had been in the non-smoking section, I might never have known she existed.

I had been to the ladies'. Peter had to slide along the bench to let me out. As I eased past him, he kissed the back of my neck.

In the toilet, I frowned at my reflection. The fluorescent lighting was doing me no favours. I looked nervous and gaunt. My hair needed trimming and my dark, floppy fringe was giving me a slightly savage aspect, as if I had something unsavoury to hide.

Business was not good. I had just moved into my office and was worried about keeping up the rent. I felt shabby.

I had got ready in a hurry that evening and was wearing my least favourite underwear. I had not had time to take a shower and shave my underarms. Peter would be presented with two ovals of harsh black stubble when we made love back at his place that night. I re-applied lipstick, wondering without humour why it was that women had underarms and men armpits. The lipstick smeared and I had to do it again.

Coming out of the ladies', I turned right instead of left and lost my way amongst the wooden booths and balconies. Distractedly, I did a full circuit around the restaurant and ended up on a raised area behind the smoking section, where the tables were empty. I turned back and my handbag slipped off my shoulder. I was bending to pick it up when I heard Sophie's voice. Our table was just the other side of the wooden divide.

'So is it love then? Come on, tell.'

Peter made a tutting noise. 'Maybe. She's very cute.'

I moved nearer to the divide. There were no speakers for the music on this side. Their voices were slightly muffled but I could probably hear them more clearly than they could hear themselves.

Alex and Sophie were making impressed *ooh* noises. Then Alex said, 'So you're at it with yet another nurse. This month's flavour of the month.' There was a pause. 'What are you going to do about Iris?'

All three of them groaned.

I felt a hollowness open up inside me, as if my guts were dissolving in acid and leaving only fumes to fill my torso. All the things I had wondered about since Peter and I met now made sense: Peter closing his study door to make phone calls; Peter always turning up late; Peter getting annoyed with me for suggesting that we met back at his place one evening and giving me an undeserved lecture about invading his personal space (something which hadn't bothered him during the first few weeks, when he got annoyed with me if I spent a night at my own flat).

He didn't need to be a good liar. I was quite capable of deceiving myself all on my own.

I scrambled to my feet just as a waitress rounded the partition with a bowl of thin, greasy French fries, piled golden-high in a tangled heap. I turned quickly. I made my way back to the ladies', then over to our table, back the way I had come.

They all smiled up at me as I approached. Peter slid out of the booth to allow me back in. As I settled into my seat, Sophie said, 'Your hair looks nice Iris, have you had it cut?'

I went through Peter's study the following morning. I was alone in the house while he walked down Lake View to the newsagent's on the main road. He was going to get some orange juice as well. I had at least twenty minutes.

There was a whole range of minor discoveries before I got to the meat of it. Firstly, there were the dirty mags in the bottom drawer of his study desk, along with two videos, the contents of which I could guess. I didn't really feel in a position to pass judgment on these. Going through somebody else's personal things is, after all, a form of pornography. Satisfying, in an illicit, guilt-inducing way, it gives you only the illusion of power. It is over too quickly and leaves a residue of self-disgust.

There was a yellow Post-It note, not stuck to anything but tucked carefully into a white envelope. Written on it in a girlish, loopy hand, was *Hope this raises a smile – you raised more than that on Thursday! Oodles of love. See you soon. M.* There was a row of X's along the bottom, about ten of them. The dots above the i's were little circles.

Then, there was the diary.

It wasn't even locked away. It was in the top drawer on the left-hand side, on top of a pile of bank statements. It was dark blue, with a hardback cover and lined pages. The last entry had been written the previous Sunday.

Boring weekend, really. Just a bit restless. Didn't do any exercise, which didn't help, other than the usual that is! I. is beginning to get a bit suspicious, I think, so I suppose I had better be on my best behaviour, unless I want some explaining to do. Had a long chat with A. on the phone and he said I should just come clean and dump her, which is easy for him to say. He's all fixed up, poor sod. Anyway, I'll feel a bastard if I hurt I.'s feelings. She's really quite sweet.

Thought A. had a point yesterday, though. Had a really nice, really long phone call from M. who sounded quite sad that I couldn't see her this weekend. It was a real pain to make my excuses and go off to meet I. in The Rising Sun, and I was late anyway which put her in one of her moods. I could tell I was in trouble as soon as I walked in the door and took one look at her face. So I got us another drink and tried to cheer her up again but all I could really think about is how it would have been much more fun to see M. who is always good for a laugh and never gets moody like I. does.

Felt so down later I couldn't get it up – not usual for me. Only way I managed it in the end was to think about talking to M. on the phone earlier that evening. I. just doesn't seem to understand my need for independence. Sometimes I think it would be less trouble just to wank off, instead of spending all that money and getting all that grief. M. got me going on the phone, describing what she was wearing when I asked. She really is very cute.

At this point there was a space and the hand changed slightly, as if he had been interrupted. I remembered that I had rung him on the Sunday evening, an hour or so after I had got home, missing him, worried because I knew that the weekend had not been a success. He had told me not to be so silly. He said he had had a great time.

There was only one other line after that:

The trouble with I. is, she has no imagination.

12

*L*ove is easy. Love is cheap. Any idiot can do it. You don't have to have brains or looks or money – you don't even have to be a nice person. Hitler fell in love – so did Stalin and Genghis Khan and Vlad the Impaler. An amoeba would weep at *Brief Encounter* (if an amoeba could weep, that is). I don't resent people who are in love. I just wish they wouldn't walk around as if it's an achievement.

So. Let us have the facts. My relationship with Peter did not end there, as it should have done. I am ashamed to say that it went on for another six months. I won't detail the tedious round of accusations – the claims and counter-claims. He was a pathological liar – but he had material to hit back with. I was paranoid.

Half of me rose from his study that day, packed my things and left his house for good, the half of me that had read the diary; but the other half, the bodily half, remained. I was split. There were two situations I could choose: the truth, and what I wanted to be the truth. One was unpleasant and dark and difficult – the other was unpleasant and dark and easy. It was then I realised that falling in love is approximate to having a frontal lobotomy.

Did I love Peter?

I loved being wanted very badly. The withdrawal of that was one of the worst things that had ever happened to me. I felt cosy with Peter and Alex and Sophie – symmetrical, rather than the thin, singular woman who sat at her desk and tapped at a keyboard and gazed at a white, swallowing screen.

Did I love him? I loved him as much as I am capable of love – and as much as I am incapable of loving myself.

Ah, yes. Personal responsibility. Just when you thought it was safe to get back under the duvet.

So, let us have the facts.

I actually knew that it was over the weekend before, when Peter was more than an hour late to meet me in The Rising Sun. If somebody is an hour late and then does not offer a grovelling apology or sufficient explanation, then you know.

It was the end of March. That weekend was the one when the clocks changed – and somehow that hour in the pub has become muddled in my mind with the hour that got lost. That evening was the tripwire.

For the first half-hour I felt resigned but hopeful. For the next half-hour, I felt stupid. People looked, pityingly. Then there was a brief five minutes or so of anger. *How dare he? He had better have a good explanation*. Then, equally briefly, I fantasised about the magnanimity I would demonstrate upon his arrival, despite my anger – and his amazement and gratitude at realising I was still here.

But there comes a point, in waiting for someone, when you realise that it has gone beyond either generosity or stupidity. You have slipped into your own little world, a world of dogged surreality. For the last twenty minutes of my wait I needed the toilet but could not go in case Peter stuck his head round the door in the meantime, saw I was not there, and left. So instead of relieving my bladder, I relieved my heart. And I did it like this.

Peter had been killed in a road accident. He had been driving along the Watford by-pass, on his way here, going at roughly sixty miles an hour, and perhaps not paying due care and attention because he was worried that he was so late, concerned that I might not wait for him, anxious because in his heart of hearts he knew that our relationship was going wrong and he had to make things right between us. He wanted that more than anything in the world. He wanted it more than life.

When I learned about his death, I would feel guilty for my anger – but even more guilty for my mistrust. The guilt and sorrow would become briefly overwhelming when, a week later, I received a letter from a solicitor inviting me to meet him at his offices in the West End at my earliest possible convenience. In my heart of hearts, I would know what was coming.

It would be hard but gradually, with the help of Peter's friends and Peter's money, I would recover. His loss would be like a pebble in my heart, a small sad lump which would never go away. But I would learn to live with it because, after all, Peter would want me to be happy. He had left everything he owned to me, after all. I would give up being an Information Consultant and set up a charity to help the unexpectedly bereaved. In my spare time, I would dabble in ceramics, or poetry perhaps. I would write an article about all of it for a broadsheet newspaper.

A lorry pulling out of a side road ahead blew a tyre, slammed on the brakes and skidded. A van in front of Peter went into the lorry. Peter went into the van. He was killed outright. The van driver was trapped for three hours; the lorry driver unscathed. It was nobody's fault.

Given the choice, which of us could honestly say that we would rather have our lover unfaithful than dead?

*

On Monday, I told Tomlinson that I wanted to move offices. I wanted a room at the front of the building, on the ground or first floor, with a heater that worked properly.

I had a lunchtime drink with George, in the Cittie of Yorke, in the snug where my panic attack had warned me that life was about to get serious. It was only a few weeks since he had told me that he was in love. This time, he sat wrapped around a pint of lager and told me that it was all over. Out of the blue and for no clear reason which she had been prepared to offer, Jerry had announced that she didn't think they were really suited. He had been dumped.

We were sitting next to each other. The pub was crowded and there was another couple opposite us. Intimate conversation was out of the question.

His left hand was resting on his thigh. I put my right hand on top of it, out of pity, out of tenderness, perhaps with a little love. He turned his own hand and clutched at mine with the ferocity of an astronaut free-floating in outer space, worried his vessel might drift off without him. He did not look at me. I knew that he was holding my hand so tightly to prevent himself from crying in public.

We sat there in silence, our undrunk drinks on the table in front of us, and listened to the couple opposite argue lightly about whether it would be best to go to Greece or Portugal that summer. Underneath the table, our hands were fused together.

I felt an odd sense of peace, despite – or perhaps because of – the fact that I was filled with overwhelming feelings of regret.

If there was a spark of some sort between George and me, now would be the time for it to ignite. I would put my arm around him, comfort him. He would turn to me. We would have a future. We knew each other well enough for that.

But it wasn't there. It never had been and never would be. We both knew it and we both knew we knew. So we sat, holding hands, jointly relieved and depressed. The truth of the matter was like a big dark block of stone and we were like limpets. We had no choice.

*

I meet him, the man, at an impromptu get-together at Susan's. It is the following weekend, Saturday night.

The official line is that we are sharing a cab home – we live in the same direction – but Susan gives me a heavy wink as she hands me my coat. In the minicab back to his place, we talk about how everyone at the party was watching us and probably knew what was going to happen before we knew ourselves.

Are all top-floor flats penthouses? My flat is on the top floor but I'm not sure you can have a penthouse in an ex-council property with small windows and a stairwell that always stinks of cat pee, even though nobody in our block owns a cat.

His flat, however, is a different matter. It is not flash or expensive, like Peter's house, but it is definitely a penthouse.

On the first level are the hallway, bedroom, kitchen and bathroom. I get the guided tour. Up a short, twisting flight of stairs is a huge sitting-room with sliding doors which lead out to a small, rectangular balcony. In the dark the view is, of course, hugely romantic: white and orange lights, golden-lit windows and blue-black squares of buildings seemingly built in heaven-ascending waves. It is like being on a ship. I had no idea such glamour was possible in East Barnet.

It is very, very late and we are both very, very drunk.

He leaves me on the balcony and goes inside to sit on the sofa, where he withdraws a tobacco tin and a packet of Rizlas and proceeds to roll a joint the size of my forearm. He brings it out on to the balcony and we are silent for a time, passing it between us, watching the view and glancing at each other occasionally with secretive, knowing smiles. Flakes of ash and paper flutter from the end of the joint and drift down, like confetti. There is no wind.

When it is finished we go back inside and he closes the sliding doors because, we both realise, it is bloody freezing. He stands before me and lifts a forefinger, solemnly. 'Music,' he says, 'and a nightcap.' He points at a wall-mounted shelf unit of CDs, behind me, then disappears downstairs.

By the time he returns with a bottle of Macallan and two glasses, I have selected some soul. He takes the CD from me and looks at it. 'Good choice,' he says approvingly.

Our first glass of Macallan goes down in one. Then we dance.

Thirty minutes later, my limbs are in revolt. I am still vertical, but only just. He is having the same problem, fortunately, and we are both hysterical with laughter. The soul has become funk and we are scuffing up the rug in front of the sofa, holding each other occasionally, then breaking apart to do our own little thing for a few bars before colliding again. He has turned the music up. He shouts above it. 'How much more dancing do we have to do before we can go to bed?'

I shout back. 'Two more tracks and one more Macallan!'

As the second track finishes we drain our glasses and look at each other.

We are poised for a moment. He has a thin line of single malt dribbling down the right side of his chin. I notice, as if for the first time, that he is incredibly, ludicrously tall, a building of a man with broad shoulders, intelligent grey eyes and a squashy nose. I feel blissfully happy and want to hit him, just to make sure he is real.

Simultaneously, we make a dash for the stairs. We reach them at the same time and he knocks against me. His weight bounces me away but I make a grab for his shirt collar. He shakes me off and, as we both hoot with laughter, careers down the stairs just ahead of me. When he reaches the bedroom, he dives for the bed from the door.

I make it as far as the door frame but know that diving is out of the question. I am as breathless as if I had been slammed up against a wall. I am still laughing but the laughter comes in wild, hysterical gulps. I feel such a spinning combination of drunkenness and exhaustion and lust that I realise that now, at this moment, I am truly mad. Reason is gone. Logic is gone. I am all corporeal. There is another human being here and he is mad too. We are nothing but sensation.

The cold hard feeling behind my shoulder blades is his bedroom wall. I am leaning back against it at an uncomfortable angle. I can feel my strength slithering down my legs so the only thing to do is let my back slide down and my limbs crumple until I am seated on the floor. I close my eyes briefly but that makes the room swing upside-down, so I open them again.

He has collapsed on the bed, flat on his back, spread-eagled. I wonder how he can stare up at the ceiling. Doesn't it make him feel sick? His right foot is close to my face and I examine the sole of his shoe, which undulates with tiny ridges.

'What do women want?' he burbles happily.

'What?' I frown at the shoe. Does he seriously expect sensible conversation out of me?

'What do women want? Someone once said ...' He pronounces someone, *zumwan*. 'Someone once said, asked, and men have been asking ever since, you see ...'

I know that if I don't stop him the night will go rapidly downhill. Using several unexpected muscles in my back, I launch myself up and off from his carpet/wall and land on the bed, which bounces slowly as I clamber slothfully up his right leg.

When I reach his groin, I give a little *hup* and end up sitting upright, straddling his waist. 'Stupid question,' I say emphatically, poking at his chest with my forefinger. His chest is very hard. 'Stupid. No such thing as *women*. Completely different. Don't generalise. It's stupid.'

He gives a terrifyingly sober smile, reaches out and takes my hand. 'OK ...' he says gently, stroking the inside of my wrist, 'what do *you* want ...'

I smile down at him. We are suddenly still.

Very, very slowly, I lower my face towards his. As I do,

his hands slide up my arms, inside my loose shirtsleeves. My shirt is silk. His touch is so light that I can scarcely decipher it from the rustle of fabric along my forearms. As my upper torso approaches his, my legs straighten out behind me so that I am lying stretched on top of him. When my face is so close to his that I can feel the soft wings of his breath, I whisper, 'Someone who'll dance with me.' And in the next moment our lips melt together and his mouth is wide and full and I am falling through space with all the bad things that have ever happened to me rushing away into infinity. There is only now.

The kiss is very long and somehow, during it, things become unbuttoned. We are clumsy. (He starts to giggle.) His arms are endless; his legs everywhere.

I clamber around him. It is like having my own private Everest.

He wraps his body around mine and pulls me in. I huddle into him, then lie still for a moment, thinking the warmest of thoughts.

I wonder whether we are going to have sex now or fall asleep.

I lift my face and am surprised to see that his eyes are open. He is looking down at me and grinning. Suddenly, we are struck again by the hilarity of our situation, a fresh moment of glee. I roll away, almost laughing. He grabs me. I wrestle back on top of him and hold his arms above his head. He makes a throaty sound of mock horror. For the sheer hell of it, I bite his nose. He grabs my shoulders and in one swift movement lifts me up into the air, clear of him, locking his arms and holding me suspended.

We gaze. His eyes shine. My teeth tug softly at my lower lip and I shake my head in wonder. We gaze some more. We cannot believe each other.

Then, very slowly, he lowers me. The warmth of his chest against mine is the warmth of the sun. My hair has tumbled over my face. He lifts it up and away and, very gently, combs his fingers through it, down around the back of my head and neck. We breathe. I slip gently sideways.

As we become sleepy I think, *I can't believe my luck*.

Three hours later, I am wide awake – the combined effect of dope and whisky, mostly whisky. I am not used to alcohol that neat. I have dehydrated quickly and, lying there, treat myself to a brief palpitation.

Next to me, my Everest is slumbering the heavy dead doze of a man who will not stir for hours. The dope and the whisky are clearly more habitual for him and, anyway, he is at home. I am in a strange land; strange man, strange bed.

For a while I lie there, my body heavy but my mind clear and awake, enjoying the strangeness.

While I have been asleep, the clocks have gone forward, so dawn is breaking early. An hour of the night has been swallowed up and summertime is bleeding through his pale curtains, filling the room with light.

The walls and the ceiling are all painted the same colour

– a creamy, uninformative beige, not very interesting but nicely done. On a chest of drawers in one corner there is a bunch of dried flowers in a blue and white vase. On the wall behind the bed, above my head, there is an empty picture hook, which both intrigues and irritates me. This could be anybody's bedroom, I think. There is nothing I can interpret.

Eventually, I become bored. I peel back the downy fullness of the duvet (nice linen, I note; off-white, crisp) and lift myself gently out of bed. The mattress creaks but the mountain does not stir. I lay the duvet back over him and stand by the bed for a moment, trying to work out how cold I am. I am wearing my silk shirt and knickers. My bra lies on the carpet beside the bed and my trousers are compressed into a crumpled cowpat on the far side of the room. I can't remember removing anything.

I button up my shirt, which is creased beyond belief, and tiptoe out of the room, pulling the door half-closed behind me but not shutting it properly in case it makes a noise. The bathroom is on the right. I sneak into it but have to leave the door ajar. I can't find the light switch and there is no window. If I shut the door I won't be able to see what I am peeing into.

Sitting on the loo, I can see the coat rack in the hallway, to one side of the front door. There is a heavy tweed coat and a dark grey trilby. Love the hat.

After I have wiped myself I stand looking down into the loo for some time, debating the relative merits of flushing.

If I do, the noise might wake him. If I don't, then he will rise later to find his toilet full. I opt for pushing the door to and flushing gently. It still makes a hell of a racket.

Rinsing my hands under the cold tap, I glance at his bathroom shelf and see a range of Clinique For Men: soap, facial wash, tonic. I am impressed. I have picked up a man who uses more expensive cosmetics than I do. Next to the soap is a grey and plum coloured bag which makes me feel suddenly sad with recognition. Peter had one. Every man I have ever slept with has had one. Men's toiletry bags are always dark grey and that heavy dried red colour that makes me think, *dead blood*. What he has gained on the soap, he has lost on the bag.

Back out in the hall I pause, listening at the bedroom door. He is still out for the count. The flat is mine to explore.

As I pass the coat-rack I grab the trilby and plonk it on my head, then pad into the kitchen like a downmarket Judy Garland, in search of fruit juice. His is not one of those kitchens where everything is disguised as a cupboard. It is long, galley-shaped and endearingly low-tech. I locate the fridge and a tall glass and pour myself grapefruit juice. As I put the carton back in the door I note the contents of the rest of the fridge: three cans of beer, a jar of red pesto sauce, a glass bowl of nectarines and some blue cheese, still sealed in its supermarket plastic. Spot the busy urban professional. In the place for eggs there is a tub of low-fat sunflower spread with the lid slightly skew-whiff. I click it into place.

I lean back against the counter while I gulp the juice. There is a cork board above the fridge. Pinned on it are a small selection of postcards, one from France, one from Bali and another with a pony on the front. There is also a photo of two young boys, aged about five and three – the regulation school picture in an oval cardboard frame. I peer at it. There is a family resemblance. I pull a face and hope they are nephews.

There is another card which has fallen off face up so I feel that it is all right to read that one. It says. *Dear Stephen – just a quick one to say thanks for all you did last weekend, it was a real help and Madge and John had a really good time, Boozy too. Tomas is going to Scotland at the end of the month so ring him before then if you want. Thanks again. Jill.* There are no kisses. I wonder if this is good news or bad.

I finish the juice and rinse the glass, then place it upturned on the drainer. I shiver. It is chilly in here but my body is all at sea. I am too tired and too thrilled and too awake to feel anything as mundane as cold.

The stairs to the sitting-room are to the left of the kitchen. After the bare linoleum, the carpet beneath my feet feels rich and thick.

The sitting-room is full of light. The bottle of Macallan and our two glasses are sitting on a low coffee table next to the sofa and the red light of the power button on the CD player is still on. I have a brief moment of nostalgia for record players. If we still used them, there would be a soft, repetitive exhalation as the needle and arm bounced gently at the end of a record. Instead, there is only a barely detectable hum. I turn it off.

Outside, a white morning has arrived, like a luxury limousine parked in the air beyond the window. I wonder what time it is; too late to pretend I am still having a date, too early to leave, although I know that I will soon. I open the sliding doors and step out onto the balcony, throwing one arm around myself as the cold air hits me and holding the trilby firmly on my head with the other. The stone tiles burn the pads of my feet and a fierce, grabbing wind flickers my shirt tails around my hips. My legs bulge instantly with goose bumps.

I gaze out across the houses, high above the dawn. The view is less romantic in daylight but still empty and quiet. The whole world is having Sunday.

I know that soon I will go back inside and shiver myself down the stairs, back to the warmth of the sleeping man with grey eyes. I know that we will make love – not this morning, probably, but soon. I know that he will be strong and good and that afterwards he will shower. He's the showering type. I also know – am quite certain – that it will not last.

But for the moment I am up here, high above everyone else, borne upwards on my merry cloud of insight and breathing in the morning. The breeze is pressing my shirt against my shaking body. I lift my face to it and close my eyes, loving myself. I dance.